THE SHELTER

PETER FOLEY

For Heiðar.
Also, for Helen: everything.

THE LAST PLANE BACK TO PARADISE

Breathe.

This is a contentious story. It's a story of possibilities and improbabilities, of decisions and change, of the moments, both powerful and forced, that pave the path to catastrophe.

You might be on this path, but don't worry, you're sure to find company. I know of at least five people heading towards disaster right now. Drew Samuel is one of them. He's thirty-two, slight build, average height, with loosely curled flaxen hair and tired olive-colored eyes. He's currently on an airplane, dressed as he usually is – in sandals, red beach shorts, an orange T-shirt, and a wool-lined denim jacket.

He's a DJ, although the days of hit songs, arena crowds, and cramped after show parties are behind him. Now, he's got uncharted albums, tiny festival stages, and Bobby, his long-serving manager of dubious repute.

Drew's future isn't set yet, but the declines of his recent past have delivered him to an unenviable present. In other words, the rigors of the road have broken his spirit. I don't know if his courage will return, but I do know this: if he maintains his seat on this airplane, a dangerous series of events will unfold.

Drew's hungover and his flight is delayed. He's made it to his seat, but his condition is deteriorating. While lively passengers mutter, he melts. Beads of sweat gather on his brow as he looks back at the last twelve hours of his life with regret.

Somebody shoot me. When will I learn? Vodka is evil... Peace and tranquility, please, God, give me peace and tranquility.

Desperate for relief from the rising cabin temperature, he reaches a trembling arm to the ceiling panel and twists the serrated air nozzle. It exhales hot air.

"Excuse me, sir," a voice says over his shoulder, "I'm afraid that can't take up a whole seat. Please stow it in the overhead compartment."

Drew flinches. *Please, no...*

Memories flash and distract: his fingers wrapped around a glass bottle, the sound of sloshing and the taste of concentrate. He blinks himself upright, banishing the caustic images, and his vision settles on a flight attendant. She's small, round, and brilliant red. A white scarf hangs from one side of her hat and tucks into her neckline somewhere. Drew can't fathom it.

The scarf? Where does it go?

He stares at her wrinkled uniform.

"Sir, stow that away, please," she says.

He wonders what she means.

Why's she so annoyed? Oh, wait, no. That. It can only be that.

Strapped into the seat next to him is a two-foot, plinth-mounted microphone with the words "**Worst DJ of 2021**" etched on the base. It absorbs his attention.

Thanks, BundaFestival, you smart-arse. I bet Bobby put you up to that.

Reality reaches him in waves, waves that smash into a million drops and scatter. His eyes wander around the plane. Passengers peek back at him.

"Sir, sir? Are you listening?" The flight attendant is not letting this go.

"I'm sorry," he says, "but I really, really want to go home."

A few passengers snigger.

Drew nods. Now he understands. Now he knows what must be done. He must stow his dubious prize in the overhead locker. *Certainly. Of course.*

He fumbles at the inscrutably smooth seat belt clip but fails to decipher its suddenly elaborate design. He pulls at its heavy nylon straps.

What's going on here? Help. Why isn't this working?

Confounded by the clinking metal, he's trapped in his chair.

"What a mess!" shouts a passenger, and others agree. Brash sneers and other antagonisms, deliberately not whispered, trample and bruise. Time distorts. The waves in Drew's mind become a stormy sea, and the flight attendant presses the issue again.

"Sir, if you can't stow that away, I'm going to call security and have you escorted off the plane."

He gasps for air. Everyone is looking and it's so hot in here – hard to breathe. Footsteps come up the aisle, he fears the worst until a familiar smile appears, and a crack of laughter breaks the tide.

"Thank God," Drew mumbles into his hands.

"Don't worry, my lovely," Bobby says to the flight attendant.

Bobby's older than Drew, yet somehow, he exudes a vitality that Drew doesn't. It's thanks in part to his smile. Bobby flashes the crowd a full-contact grin, complete with sharp teeth, fleshy gums, and glinting sea-blue eyes.

No one can weaponize a smile like Bobby. He'd have made a fantastic pirate.

"I'm sorry I'm late," Bobby says. "Don't worry, ma'am. I'm this man's manager. Allow me to deal with this." Bobby crouches to Drew's eye level.

"Hey, Drew. Drew? Your award's going in the overhead, OK? You haven't been the same since Berlin, have you, lad, but don't worry, it's been a long three months, but the tour's over and you're going home, yeah?"

Drew feels a slow, leery frown pour out of his face. Bobby stows away Drew's ill-advised metal mascot and turns to the flight attendant.

"I'm so sorry, dear, it's clear what's happened here – this man has had a bad oyster. The flight will do him good."

She rolls her eyes and walks down the aisle.

"What would I do without you, Bobby, my fine Irish friend?" Drew stumbles over his words. "For the last ten years, what would I have done? I'd have probably been happy and sober, I expect."

Bobby takes his seat next to Drew and leans in close, "Come on, lad. The way you behave, you'd be in the rubber room or locked up someplace without me."

"Bollocks. This is all your fault. I blame you, your stupid tour, your stupid award – and your awful vodka. Why do you always get me into this mess?"

"Sounds like you want another bottle, pal!" Bobby slaps his leg and bursts into laughter. "Some DJ you are. Mr. Superstar, my arse! You should just be grateful we got on this flight. After ten years of service as your manager, it doesn't hurt to say thanks once in a while."

"Thanks for the last ten years of shitty economy flights and arsehole-of-nowhere festivals and generally career-ending shit bookings, *Bobby*," Drew leers.

"Don't mention it."

Drew sighs.

"And you should be extra thankful for this particular flight. You know my brother's a pilot, right? Well, he's been briefed that all flights to California are being grounded as of tomorrow. A hurricane's due in – Hurricane Jason – and it's going to be a big one, so we have to get home and batten down the hatches until it passes."

"A hurricane in California? You're full of crap, Bobby." Drew nods again until another wave of vodka rears up at him.

More mutters and sniggers from the other passengers, but Drew can't hear them now. He pushes himself deep into the chair's smooth squeaky leather.

It's finally over. After three months, no more tour buses, no more flights, no more half-empty festivals, no more Bobby, and definitely no more eastern European booze. Just this one plane ride and it's all over. I've finally made it.

The plane thrusts down the tarmac and lifts Drew into a cloudless night. He tries to banish a harsh ringing from his ears. In 30,000 feet of sky, he blinks himself into a turbulent sleep. At five hundred miles an hour, he flies unconscious into the eye of a new storm.

BLUE MONDAY

That's a shame. It seems that dark luck stirs a distinct and unfortunate future for us, but we'll face it together. While Drew rests, we'll seek another star in our galaxy; we'll search for Hazel Cox; may she fare better. She's of more obvious substance, which is to say, she's a healthy rational human being with many of the contemporary human traits: humor, health, strength, desire, and fear that her best days are gone. She wonders if life could have more satisfaction, more delight. Indeed, it could, but even though Hazel's one of the brightest lights in our sky, the twinkle of her star is about to dim behind a dangerous new cloud.

Hazel takes a cool sip of Sauvignon Blanc, and lets the sun carry her spirits to the sky on a current of warm beach air.

Welcome to the bright bleached wooden deck of the Wolf and Cellar beach bar, Santa Monica, California. Hazel, Lara and Sissy meet here every Sunday afternoon and get giddy loud among the palm trees and surfboards.

"I agree with Hazel. You're the *worst*," Lara says to Sissy.

Sissy laughs. "Oh really? Remember the last time you hooked up on Tinder? That encounter's still on Pornhub."

"Shut up! And no, it's not," Lara says. "Besides, I'm a kept woman these days."

"Going well, is it?" Hazel tops up her glass from a chilled, dripping bottle.

"We're quite the domestic couple now," Lara says. "Kurt's at home right now fixing the sink."

"Oh!" Hazel and Sissy say.

"What?"

"You never learn," Hazel says. "Remember the last time Kurt tried DIY? He tried to replace a shingle and fell through the roof."

"God, I know. Don't tell his parents. They'd kill him!" Lara says. "He had to hide his limp all through Thanksgiving – it was so funny. Anyway, enough about me – for now – let's come back to me, but right now, I want to know about my gorgeous Hazel. Anyone special on your radar?"

"Here we go again… every week." Hazel rolls her eyes and turns towards the sea. "Isn't that beautiful? Why don't we ever talk about *that*?" She points at the beach. "That view is why I love this place. You can see all the way to the beach and over the ocean."

"Excellent conversation changing skills as always," Sissy says, laughing into her oversized glass. "Hazel, we love you, you know we love you, but you've been single for too long. You need to get out there and have some fun."

Hazel lets a mild wave of taunts wash over her while she takes in the view of the coarse golden sands. Across the beach, a group of surfers carry their boards across the frothy water's edge, and a happy-looking couple embrace in the warm crystal sea.

A phone rings.

"Oh! Somebody's getting a call – a booty call!" Lara says.

Hazel looks at her phone. The screen reads: Flynn.

"Don't do it!" Lara says.

"I have to."

"You're breaking the golden rule!" Sissy says.

"Exactly," Lara says. "Never answer the phone to your boss on the weekend. It can't be good!"

"I hate my job." With a sigh and a swipe, Hazel answers the call.

"Hazel? It's Flynn. Look, cancel all your appointments for the foreseeable. I need to see you first thing. We have a situation."

It's Monday, 8 am, and barely an echo of the weekend remains.

I need to win the lottery so I can avoid this Monday crap altogether.

Hazel always walks to work. She reaches the end of a hot sidewalk, removes her shoes, and steps onto the beach. This route to work adds fifteen minutes to her commute, but it's worth every second. The sun floats like a golden honey drop, and she can feel its heat under her pantsuit and the warmth of the sand on the soles of her feet.

She walks into the office barefoot, leaving behind pronounced broken footprints of sand on the front-desk carpet and the elevator floor. She dusts her feet off at her desk and slips into her shoes as the sun paints a thick copper rectangle on her wall to declare the morning fully accomplished.

Tying her lightly curled hair back, she sits at her sparse government-issue desk, on which resides a computer and nothing more. Other employees decorate their workspaces like college dorms, with vinyl record sleeves propped up, novelty license plates stamped with "It's five o'clock somewhere", or dozens of boxed Star Wars figurines and other banal treasures, but Hazel likes her desk clean and noncommittal. It's a simple, easy-to-control space that would normally provide peace and quiet, but not today, not in Flynn's company.

Flynn is the head of administration at CeTech Weather Services, the government's leading meteorology research center. He's a round-faced, square-shouldered man with thick graying hair, nice enough as bosses go, but his way of swallowing hard and waving his hand before he speaks annoys Hazel to the point of distraction. It looks like he's working on a difficult bowl of oatmeal while trying to swat a fly. This motion is particularly prominent when Flynn's about to say something he's very pleased with.

Uncomfortable in her chair, Hazel gives Flynn her best diplomatic repose and an accidental reflexive sigh.

"Look, we've known about this storm for days. Last week, I went back over the last thirty-two years of California's atmospheric infrared data, that's nearly three million weather-related data points every single day. And from what I've seen, yes - Hurricane Jason will be an unusual weather event for California. But the media are telling people it will last three weeks - that's crazy. It'll be bad, but it won't wash the world away. Two to three days tops, and the hurricane will have run its course."

Hazel can see Flynn is weary of the same old arguments. He perches on her desk like a pile of work, rubbing his gray eyebrows and adjusting his eyeglasses.

"So, you're saying we should just ignore all the media discussions?" he says. "And we have nothing to worry about? Great! Great advice from my top researcher, thanks. I'll take it to the press immediately." He pauses. "Dammit. They're going to eat me alive. They have a bug up their ass about this hurricane – a big bug! Maybe it's been a slow news week, but–"

"Flynn! I'm not saying it isn't anything to worry about – we have plenty to worry about. Even in a median case scenario, under these conditions the streets will be heavily flooded, power outages will occur, people will be cut off and stranded, and lives will be lost. That's why I'm recommending military support standing by with emergency aid, and I suggest we ask for extra funding from the federal government to coordinate the state's preparedness and response. I'm not saying that we should build Noah's ark! Three days tops, and this thing will blow over."

"Don't talk about the federal government like it's so easy." Flynn's eyes widen. "The President doesn't like California very much since we pushed back on the emissions and water guidelines. We have to talk this hurricane up just to get basic assistance from the administration. Besides, *sources,* mostly online redneck media outlets, are telling the White House that the hurricane will be a big one, way bigger than anything we have seen before – it's Judgment Day, according to these people. Even the President is saying it's going to be 'huge' and 'phenomenal' and 'the biggest hurricane you have ever seen' and 'biblical' and 'incredible' and 'beautiful'. Those were his actual words."

"He would say that, wouldn't he?" she says. "But based on what *evidence*?" She shakes her head at the floor. At only twenty-nine, she's tired of these pre-coffee battles.

"It beats me, but look," Flynn takes off his glasses, "I've been asked if you can play their tune on this one - big hurricane, blah, blah, just–"

"I'll do no such thing. You know me better than that. I can't go on TV and lie to the entire state!"

"If you're right, then the hurricane is gone in two or three days, it's a win, but if you're wrong and it goes on beyond that, the White House is right. In either case, if we just play along we win, and everyone was prepared. Just do a TV and maybe a radio appearance and sing along with the federal line. It might not be ideal, it might not be very scientific, but at least this way we keep our funding. Think about it. We know one thing for sure – a big hurricane is coming, and it's coming our way."

The wall clock ticks. Hazel's aversion to arguments kicks in and she has nothing more to say.

"Good," Flynn says, swallowing oatmeal and swatting a fly. "Now, I have the interviews lined up for you. The usual TV, possibly radio. Remember, big hurricane, blah, blah. It's all lined up, and don't worry – when the interviews are over, you can wait it out in the government safe house at the Staples Center. Oh, come on, Hazel, cheer up and play along. What's the worst that can happen?"

WHAT WOULD JOHN THINK?

Drew wakes abruptly with a surprisingly difficult snore.

Where the hell am I?

He looks around. "Ahh, home sweet home. Finally, back in my own bed. Malibu, I've missed you."

With a roll and a fall, he's relieved of his bed. He sweeps past the empty cans of cider and heads to the bathroom to check on the progress of a nervous tic he'd developed on tour, after Berlin. The spasms manifest as an involuntary tensing of his right cheek, resulting in the appearance of him narrowing one eye as if bracing for an imminent slap.

I look so lopsided these days.

He puts on his bathrobe and presides over the morning traffic from the comfortable vantage of his bedroom window. Looking through the glass, and through the cherry blossom tree that grows on the other side, he can see past the courtyard to a road full of slow-moving traffic.

The tightly packed line of vehicles sits below a blue sky as shadow blossoms move across his apartment floor. He loves this tree. Its petals hover like a delicate pink cloud above its slender trunk. Its forked branches reach up like arms, stretch up towards his window and playfully touch, tap, and tease the air back and forth, all the while sheltering him from the morning heat.

The birds seem quiet today, and soon the traffic and the charm of morning fades.

One homemade breakfast burrito later, Drew's coffee has cooled, much like the spirit in his apartment. His unfortunate metal mascot – the two-foot microphone – sits on a heap of unpacked suitcases by the door. Unpacking seems like hell, so he doesn't bother.

After three months of carting these cases around Eastern Europe, it would be easier just to burn them at this point.

He knows that one – the heavy yellow hard-shell case with the broken wheel – is packed full of dirty laundry. The small red case – the one with the ribbon on the handle – is full of keepsakes found on his travels: AAA backstage passes; a gold-colored six-page emergency passport; various inflight magazines; a soccer shirt from FC Dynamo Kyiv, a drumstick given to him by a band he saw but can't remember who, and the hospital tag he acquired in Berlin.

After three months of being away, Drew's finally home, but he has no clue how to enjoy the sympathetic surroundings beyond playing a few Beatles records, drinking decaf, and making impulsive online purchases, the last of which is about to arrive by mail, delivered by Grahame, his fat, flat-footed, friendly neighborhood mailman. Drew swings open his door like a man who hasn't seen company in an age.

"Hey! Grahame! How's it been?"

"Hey buddy. Long-time no-see. So, you're finally back from your vacation? You got all the packages I left for you on your porch?"

"Yeah, I did. You got another for me?"

"It's more than one," Grahame lifts the strap of his mailbag off his pooch belly, and with friendly dismay hands over several parcels. "You really need to lay off drinking when you're online."

"Yeah, but for the record, going on tour is no vacation, not these days."

Grahame chuckles. "Oh, it must be hard pressing play on a Spotify playlist every night. Anyway, I hope you've got a plan for the terrible weather coming."

Drew looks skyward at the rich California blue.

"I know it looks nice up there right now," Grahame says, "but they say it's due to change today."

"Who says?"

"Have you seen a newspaper recently?"

"You know I've been in Europe for months."

Grahame rolls his eyes and hands Drew today's press. "Jason, it's called. A big hurricane, like Katrina but worse, at least that's what some are saying. You never know who to believe with this stuff. Today even hurricanes are political. Republicans say it's going to be watery hell and the Democrats disagree yet still want to blame the President because of a reduction in storm-protection spending last year – blah, blah, blah."

"Yeah, OK, thanks, G."

"I'll be seeing you, Drew. Oh, and FYI - This is my last day on the job till the hurricane passes, and all public services are suspended from noon. Oh, and let me guess," he says, turning to leave, "…you bought another John Lennon cassette tape, right?"

Drew has no idea.

How much did I spend this time?

Tearing into one brown padded envelope, he shouts to the mailman, "No, it's…" he says, scanning the parcel contents, "It's… oh, for crying out loud!"

Grahame chuckles in the distance as Drew looks over his newest copy of *Imagine* featuring the Flux Fiddlers.

"I bet John would be livid with me. I now own nine copies of this damn cassette tape with no way of playing them. *Imagine no possessions.* Sorry, John."

He checks out the newspaper, its headline reads: "California unprepared as Hurricane Jason looms in the Pacific." Glancing over the top of the page, he watches Grahame turn a corner as a woman jogs into the courtyard. His heart accelerates and he waves nervously.

"Come on, Drew," he says under his breath. "After years of waving across the courtyard, it's finally time to have an actual conversation with a neighbor. You can do this. Yes, she's hot, and I'm not sure how we get from 'Hey, some hurricane, huh?' to 'So dinner tonight?' but man up, this is going to go well."

He walks over as the jogger stops and begins her cooldown routine, which, combined with her flowing auburn hair, stops the words in Drew's mouth. She's tall, toned with disciplined posture and she looks like an athlete in her tight-fitting running gear. Drew realizes he hasn't run for anything, aside for an occasional airport gate in a decade.

"Um. Hi, Megan." He waves his paper. "So, some hurricane, huh?" He suddenly remembers how rough he looks in his bathrobe. He glances down and grimaces.

"Ugh! I'm so sick of hearing about it. It's all people have been talking about for the last two weeks."

"Really?"

"Where have you been? The moon?"

"I've been on tour… I'm a DJ, so…" Drew says hazily. He watches Megan stretch and manages to keep the conversation alive with a mumble. "…So, where do you jog?"

"Just around Baker, Simmons Street, then a few laps of Julian Park. It's about 5k," she says, mid toe touch.

"Nice, I think I'd like to spend some time at a park, is it far from here?"

"It's literally four blocks away from your apartment." Megan moves into a calf stretch, pushing against her apartment wall. "Yeah. How long have you lived here?" she says.

"I left Liverpool and moved here about two and a half years ago."

She nods. "You have a strong accent."

"Thanks. When I first came over, I lived in the Sunset Tower hotel for a few months - you know that place? It's where John Wayne brought a cow up to his penthouse, and Truman Capote called it 'Posh' and said that 'It's where every scandal that ever happened, happened'. These days the most scandalous thing at that place is the price of coffee at the Starbucks across the street." He trails off as Megan turns into a side stretch, but he finds fresh momentum.

"So, the hurricane. What are your plans?" he says, refocusing.

"I'm going to a place upstate, it's like a big bunker up in the hills – has a huge inventory of supplies. I'm going to settle down there."

"Can't you just stay indoors here? Batten down the hatches or something…"

"You're kidding, right? If it's going to be Katrina times ten, I'm not sitting here. A few feet from the sea is not a good place to be during a hurricane unless you want to be a sitting duck for Judgment Day. It'll be coming at us from right over there," she points at the beach, "so I'm heading to higher ground."

"Sure."

"Yep."

"OK… So, where's this place you're going?"

She shakes her head and pulls a note out of her jogging belt. "Here's the address and a map. I have lots of copies, in every bag, every room, and in my car. I don't want to be caught off guard if the hurricane arrives early." She pauses. "I suppose, if you've got nowhere else to go, you should check it out." She goes into her apartment and leaves Drew looking at the heavily folded note. It's a map. It takes him a few moments to decipher it.

I know this place…

The day moves on rapidly, a little too rapidly, so Drew takes himself off to the beach. It's a short walk from his apartment, and it takes him past a well-liked coffee place, the only one he knows.

California in the springtime is airy and warm. Yellows and blues are dotted with high lilting palms that wave and shine glossy green. He sits on the yellow sand with a hot latte in hand and watches the green feathers of the palms recline one hundred feet overhead. The green bursts in the blue, and a full moon lingers in the sky like an X-ray.

He breathes in the ocean air.

Peace at last.

He watches a man and woman jog together along the beach.

They look successful. They have all the proper jogging clothes on and everything, as if they've just run off the cover of a lifestyle magazine. They look happy, too. Bet they jog together every day, have a routine. Wonder what that's like. I bet it's nice... What the hell am I doing here?

He looks at the horizon and occasionally back at the pair of distant joggers as the first drops of rain fall lightly on the sand. He starts to think seriously about the situation as an old man walks past him, smiling and carrying a sign that reads, 'Don't worry, Salvation is Waiting'.

4

THE THIRD MEMBER OF OUR CLUB

"Stephen! How's our blue-eyed boy?"

Stephen stands at his raw timber desk and smiles at his laptop while simultaneously trying to organize his papers and tuck in his shirt. A gentle breeze flows through his small woodshed-turned-office, lifting sawdust into the air and scattering pencils to the floor.

"I'm doing great, Mr. Johnson, just great," Stephen says as he discreetly retrieves a crumpled sheet of paper from his waistline.

"Excellent. Do we have everyone on this video call? William, are you with us?"

"Yes." Mr. Johnson's younger brother, William, a smaller, but similar-looking man, appears on the screen beside his brother. Together, they form the complete visage of Stephen's Two-Headed Boss.

"Good, good," says the older Mr. Johnson, whose large shiny head is even more incredible on-screen than in person. "So, William and I wanted to have a little chat with you. We've been talking about the fall line-up, and we've decided that we need some new product ideas to really juice things up again this year, just like you did last fall with the hedgehog house design."

Stephen adjusts his hair, having noticed himself on screen.

19

"Well, sir, that was a good deal for the company and a good deal for the hedgehogs."

"Indeed. I think we sold nine thousand units last year?"

"Not far off," William says, "The 'hog house idea has been good for us, a great seller for the past two quarters. So, allow me to say that your work here is much appreciated, Stephen, and we're obviously keen for that to continue."

"Yes, good point. OK, let's get to that first," the other Mr. Johnsons says. "Stephen, Derek Crumbles and I had a little conversation last week. You know Derek Crumbles, don't you?"

"Er… He runs the yard division at C-brim."

"And he's our number one competition when it comes to yard products. Mr. Crumbles gave me some surprising news about a conversation you had with him recently. Apparently, you had talks with him about leaving us and joining C-Brim?"

"It was just an email…" Stephen struggles to find the words.

"Look, Stephen, I want you to know that your exemplary skills and ideas are valuable, and the only place to monetize them is right here at The Shed. You've already had a number of wonderful pay raises since you started as a grunt cutting timber for us a few years back, and we feel that your loyalty is due. Now, I've had a discussion with Mr. Crumbles, and he's no longer in the hiring mood. Understand?"

"Yes, Mr. Johnson."

"So, the fall line-up, it's just turning spring, and we need ideas locked and loaded asap. You've got a week to show me something good, OK? I need you to wow me."

"I have some ideas I could walk you through right now." Stephen ruffles his papers.

Mr. Johnson glances at his watch. "I best get back to the golf course. Let's resume this tomorrow at 10 am. Have a PowerPoint ready."

"OK, Mr. Johnson, speak to you then."

Stephen ends the call shaking his head. Closing the laptop, he looks to Larry, who's been taking a smoke break by the door.

"PowerPoint? You know anything about that stuff?'

'Nope.'

'Ah, I'm never going to get rich in this place. I'm destined to have money. I deserve it."

"Get over yourself,' Larry says. "You're a grunt, just like me, and you always will be. What else is there to do in this town anyway? At least you don't have to drive the forklift all day like me. Look - my ass is getting sores! You got it better than the rest of the guys, you got your health, you got your stupid face, and you got some beer money - what more is there to have? Anyway, another pay raise would only make Muchnik hate you even more."

"Screw that guy." Stephen says in a reflex action. "That reminds me," he checks his watch, "I've got a meeting with that fat-ass about now. I deserve a pay raise just for putting up with his crap. Wish me luck."

"Good luck, and remember, he's the boss, *your* boss, so don't be an A-hole, OK?"

Stephen holds out his arms. "I make no promises." He walks from his annexed workshop to The Shed's main warehouse.

Inside the large, noisy, dimly lit main building, something new is happening. There are four, maybe five guys in blue "SecurCo" overalls climbing up ladders and running cables to different parts of the building.

"What's all this?" Stephen shouts above the din of circular saws. Muchnik, a squat man with a flabby face, waves him over.

"We're installing fifty-three new security cameras across the site. And we're improving the lighting, so the cameras perform better. These cameras are full 4K resolution, and they have a thirty-meter zoom," Muchnik says.

Cameras are being installed over every work bench, down every corridor, and in every storeroom. There appears to be no escape from the all-seeing eye.

"And the cameras are going in your shed, too, Stephen."

"So, this is what the profits from nine thousand hedgehog houses buy you? Fifty-three security cameras up your ass? Don't you think this is excessive? I mean, come on. You can't spy on people all the time."

"I can. And so can Knocker. As head of security, it's Knocker's responsibility to monitor the cameras. He'll have access to the security app so he can monitor the staff – I mean the site, 24/7."

"We already have random security searches every day and a metal detector at the door to make sure no one smuggles a pillar drill out in their shorts. And you already hired your brother as the head of security. Isn't that enough? This place is hardly a crime hotspot. You're paranoid. You'd happily let your pervert brother spy on us while we crap, wouldn't you? Where is he? We got to talk about this."

"My brother is not a pervert, and that's abusive behavior, insubordination. That's a verbal warning on your permanent record. I'm stamping down on all of this. And it's no concern of yours where my brother is. You're an employee, just like everyone else in here, so follow my rules or hit the bricks."

"Your brother's asleep in his car again, isn't he?"

Motioning no more interest in the conversation, Muchnik walks away and into his office.

Across the parking lot, there's a foot sticking out of the passenger window of Knocker's car.

"Larry! Get over here with that forklift. I need to borrow it for a second," Stephen shouts.

Larry drives over and darts out of the seat.

"Watch this." Stephen jumps in and the tires squeal as his boot hits the gas pedal. He drives to the side of Knocker's Cadillac and, being careful not to wake the man inside, sets the forks between the cars wheels. Looking to Larry, Stephen puts a finger over his mouth and shushes the crowd that's gathered outside the warehouse. With perfect poise, he drives slowly forward, easing the forks under the car, but the whirl of the hydraulic lifting cylinders is not subtle. The noise causes the sleeping foot to flinch.

Knocker bolts upright and looks out of the window with dream-like amazement as his car rises into the air. His cursing triggers laughter from the warehouse.

"What's going on! What are you doing? Stephen, you asshole!"

Knocker swings a fist out of the window towards Stephen, but now he's well above head height, and he misses his target by several vertical feet. He reaches for his cell and shouts into it. Muchnik sprints out of his office with his phone pressed to his ear, just in time to see Stephen place Knocker's car on top of the red storage container in front of the main building.

"I guess he's got a good view to keep an eye on things from up there, eh, Muchnik?" Stephen leaps out of the forklift.

"You're a madman!" Larry says, grinning at the lofted car. "You better get out of here. Look at Muchnik – he's having a shit-fit!" Larry laughs uncontrollably. The other grunts of The

Shed howl, sputter, and crease with laughter as Muchnick turns apoplectic and purple.

"Stephen," shouts Muchnick, "Get your ass out of here. You're fired!"

"Of course, I am. Screw this place and screw this town," Stephen says. "I'm done and gone.'

'Where to?' Larry says.

'Hell, I don't know… Hollywood. I'll be in touch for a reference. Adios, dickheads."

Stephen jumps into his pickup and screeches out of the parking lot.

"California, here I come!"

5

SOMEWHERE BETWEEN GOD AND JOHN WAYNE

Stephen turns up the volume on his Hank Williams playlist. Songs about rambling men, whiskey, honky-tonk women, and lonesome hearts are perfect for the twenty-two-hour 1,409-mile impulsive drive from Texas to California.

A solitary burst of early summer has appeared and promises new life to the land. On days like this, a mirage hovers above the blacktop, and the horizon is a hot line spanning three hundred and sixty degrees. It holds down a vast, empty wilderness, and the only sign of movement is the undulating telephone poles fixed by the roadside. Stephen's pickup makes good progress in the heat. There's no work here – no security checks, and there's certainly no bosses here.

Mile after mile, Stephen's mind wanders through the backroads of his mind. Memories hover and dance like butterflies, apart from one. One stands like a tombstone.

Mary. This is the first time I've left Texas since Mary.

Her name is a time machine. It sends him back nine years to high school, where he and Mary first met. St John's High didn't elect a homecoming king or queen, but if they did, Stephen and Mary would have been elected by a landslide.

She'd have hated that.

From the moment he saw her green eyes, tousled red hair, and denim shorts, he knew she was trouble, especially on hot nights after a six-pack of Best Maid Sour Pickle. but now, all that remains from those days is the old pickup truck he's driving.

She'll be long gone by now, I reckon. She probably moved up to Houston.

He shakes his head and strokes the hair out of his eyes.

She's probably married and arguing with some poor sucker right now. I hope she stayed in Texas, at least.

He laughs.

I'm not sure any other place could handle her.

He sighs.

In the distance, left and right, patches of grass move by slowly. The steering wheel jitters on a stretch of coarse road, and there's no wind apart from that which the pickup breaks. Stephen shakes his head and admires the peace, not thinking anymore, just looking at the road ahead and listening to the soft thunder of his engine and the roll of his tires on hot asphalt.

The drive was going well, until Bakersfield. In Bakersfield, there are hundreds, maybe thousands of cars sitting in the outbound lane, mile after mile, fender to fender. He thinks back, and since around Mojave County he's been the only car headed into California. That should have been a warning sign. Curiosity eventually gets the better of him, and he turns on the radio to catch the latest local traffic news. He scans the dial and settles on the first station he finds:

"This is DriveTime with KBBLBBL, brought to you by Father's Meat and Grill *Mature meat at rare prices*! I'm Vance Trick, and we're going live to the phone lines. We want to know what your hurricane plans are and whether you think Armageddon is coming to California. Ha-ha. Our first caller is Ralph. Top of the morning to you, Ralph. You're *live*!"

"Hi, this is Ralph. How are you guys?"

"We're doing good, thanks, no clouds in my sky today. How about you?"

"OK. I'm a first-time caller, but I've been listening since you were on college radio, you remember the Monkey Game? JBL campus? That's how old *I* am."

"Ah-ha! Memories, memories. We couldn't get away with that outside college! WHATSUPP!"

"Yeah, I know, right? WHATSUPP! Haha. Well, so, this Hurricane Jason, ya know, it's all going to blow over, ya know. First thing they said was it was nothing to worry about. Then it wasn't even goin' to happen, then it was going to blow itself out in the Pacific. Now they want us to panic? I tried to drop my kids off at school today, but they're closed due to the weather! C'mon!"

"I hear ya, I hear ya, I do. So, that was Ralph. He thinks it's all a storm in a teacup, a pretty sunny teacup right now, as I look outside our studio window – but is that likely

27

to change for the worse? Edith, you're on the line."

"Hi, Vance. I'm calling to say that this whole thing is so *scary*. I'm packing up my car and heading to Eastbourne, Texas. I figure I should go visit my sister until this thing is over. She has a small ranch, it's nice, but she's getting on in years, and you know how it gets, the llamas can be difficult to chase at her age. My nephew, he's a law enforcement officer, and he says he's been briefed that they're going to evacuate the State. Now, my Joey's a good kid, and he wouldn't lie to me, not to his Aunt MooMoo, so if he says it, it's true. And have you seen what's on the Facebooks? My Sara's always on that – she says the Chinese have built a radar that turns clouds into hurricanes with 5G radiation. Why is no one talking about that? And the Democrats–"

"Sorry, Edith, as you can hear, the music's coming in and that's my cue to cut to the ads. I do want to make time for all of ya, so stand by. I'll be right back after this message from our sponsor."

Here at Pastor's Meat and Grill we love Christmas, but why only thank Christ once a year? We've condensed the spirit of Christmas into a sauce we know you're going to love, all year round!

Jingle-Jingle all the way – Bring Christmas to any barbecue with Pastor's sacred sauce. It's like Christmas in your mouth!

"OK, we are back! How about that sauce, eh? Get some on your meat. Anyway, I have a text here from Adam. He says, 'I see my neighbors boarding up their windows and moving valuables to the attic. What's the point? A direct hit is going to wipe us out anyway, so why bother?' That's a good point, Adam, good point. Now, back to the callers. Ben, is that you on the line?"

"Yeah, it's me."

"OK, what do you have for us *live* here on KBBLBBL?"

"I'm sitting here, and where I am there's not a cloud in the sky, so where is it? Where's Jason? It's all a conspiracy by the media. It's fake news, and shame on you for taking part in it. It's just another lefty attempt to weaken our economy under this president."

"Sorry you feel that way, Ben, but last I heard, the weather can change, so keep your eyes on the skies!"

"Well, I've taken the precaution of stocking up on the essentials, food, water, toilet roll, just in case. I have enough supplies to wait out an ice age."

"That's good for you. I hope you left something on the supermarket shelves for me! Thanks for the call, Ben. This is KBBLBBL bringing you the hurricane live to wherever you are, and whoever you are."

Stephen turns off the radio, "Sound like bullshit to me," and doubles down on his route to Sunset Boulevard.

6

WHERE ARE THE STEAKS?

It's strange that biblical storms in the modern era always wipe out the supermarkets first. Every F-Mart in California is breaking under the pressure of Hurricane Jason, even before the gale-force winds have begun. Inside each large, brightly lit store, people hurry down aisles, leaving only a scattering of items behind. In place of common groceries like bread, pasta, beans, meat, or toilet paper, you'll likely find a special offer on disappointment and empty shelves. Let's stop by the F-Mart on Whittier Boulevard, East Los Angeles, and observe.

Courtney Weaver is browsing the aisles with her husband, Ethan.

"I've never seen so many empty shelves – it's insane," Courtney says. "I don't understand. Why is it when people think it's the end of the world, the first thing they worry about is wiping their ass?"

"I know. And it's not just toilet paper. It's like, *quick! There will never be beans again! Buy all the beans! Beans are power now!* And it's funny what people leave behind." Ethan holds up a can of spruce barley and poses with it as a disgruntled-looking man hurries past with a cart piled high with crates of beer. "That guy's going to drink his way out of this. Oh, by the way, how are we going to wipe *our* ass?"

"Your mom's on toilet roll duty. When she's out and about this week, she'll buy what she finds for us."

"Cool."

The young couple push their scantly stocked shopping cart down what once was the bread aisle. Finding nothing, they search an impoverished but still-busy meat section.

"So, my company lost most of its operating capital today," Ethan says. "Well, seventy-five percent of it and I'm relying on the online sales team's numbers to keep us afloat." His eyes run across the empty shelves.

"OK…" Courtney says, encouraging him to elaborate.

Outside the store, the night grows restless with rain.

"All public events are cancelled for the next three months. In all my years, I've never seen an overreaction like it. I have no way to support a public events company that can't put on public events for three months. I need half a million a month just to break even. I don't have reserves of gold in the Swiss Alps, you know." He directs Courtney's attention to an F-Mart employee pushing a pallet of toilet paper down a neighboring aisle, "Let's see if we can bag us some toilet paper here?"

"OK, but it's a waste of time," Courtney says, following Ethan to the pallet. "Oh my God!" She yelps. "Some people are savages."

People leap on the stacked pallet as a distressed F-Mart employee looks on. They claw at the plastic outer wrapping in a muted, brutal moment. As soon as a twelve-pack of rolls come free from the pallet's clingy grasp, hands scratch and compete for it. The action pauses when the store's lights falter and blink, triggering gasps in the dark. The horde pick up the pace, and each person rips a piece away until nothing is left but a plastic pallet and a pile of Saran Wrap.

"Ugh, this is boring. Let's get out of here," Ethan says.

"We have no chicken! I practically live on chicken and I've had to sub for frozen shrimp," Courtney says. "Anyway... the company?"

"Yeah. Don't worry. This is all just a moment in time. We're strong enough to tough this out, I think, although a lot aren't. I know companies that are either out of business already or will be by the end of the month. I have a few things they don't – great support from the bank, for example. I'm going to have to take out a bridging loan to cover the losses, but there's a small chance the government may offer a bailout. There's an announcement tomorrow about our industry. Either way, it's hard, but I need to keep my staff because when the dust settles on this, the entire world will be up for grabs. It'll be huge, and we'll be in pole position. Until then, it's tough. Oh, and making friends with the local government officials last year was a smart move. They've been supportive."

The rain becomes loud. Heavy staccato drops beat down on the metal-roofed, single-story building. It's enough to make shoppers look at each other in bemusement.

The couple cut their losses and head for the checkout. Ethan starts bagging at the counter and smiles at the checkout clerk, "So, you must've seen a lot of crazy people buying hundreds of packs of toilet paper."

The noise of a revving engine grows dangerously loud and the glass storefront explodes. A blizzard of glass shards rains down on the shoppers as an alarm starts. People drop to their knees, the rain blows through a large, jagged hole in the store where the blue SUV has come to a stop.

A man in a balaclava jumps out of the driver's side. Tattoo's run up his arms.

"Don't fucking move!" he yells. "Lay down and nobody gets hurt! This store and everything in it belong to me now."

Three men clutching rifles climb out of the car.

"Shit! Ethan, get down. We have to get out of here!" Courtney diverts her attention away from the guns. "Ethan! Ethan!"

Pushing the shopping cart out of her way, she falls to her knees and crawls toward her husband. He's lying on the floor, blood pouring from his face, a large shard of glass protruding from his head. His eyes are frozen open, he's gasping for air.

"Ethan!"

He doesn't move. He doesn't answer. Thick, dark blood streams from between his brows. Courtney steadies his head and cries for help, but with the emergency services reduced due to the hurricane, she knows help will not quickly be found anywhere in California.

Moments fade in and out. She wipes a palmful of blood away from Ethan's face. The checkout clerk yells to colleagues for help, but Courtney can't make out her words. People gather, Ethan's eyes close, someone tries CPR, but hope slips away against a backdrop of panic and looting, and Courtney's heart breaks as the rain pours in at checkout number five.

7

RIDERS ON THE STORM

Welcome to The First Temple of the People. At the Simmons Street entrance, you can hear the hum and chatter of the expectant congregation inside. Walking through the large wooden entrance, you feel the excitement of three hundred people wash over you like warm summer air. People in their smartest clothes stand and talk with good smiles and better humor as an organ band plays an upbeat melody.

Oscar, a willowy young man with neat hair and an oversized blue suit, welcomes you with a handshake. "Feel free to take a seat, stand, talk, sway, clap and please sing along,' he says. 'Newcomers are most welcome."

A sweet floral fragrance in the air can mean only one thing; Oscar's mother has arrived. She embraces her boy and steps back to get a better view of him.

"You're so tall now! When did you get this tall?" she says. A long coat hangs off her shoulders, and her gloved hands hold Oscar's.

"To think they almost took you away from me and put you in jail."

"I know, mom, I know."

The church interior is a modest open room with a low white ceiling. There are no windows, and the walls are blank, but it's a well-maintained utilitarian space that's now rich in animation and faith. People pack the house, standing and dancing around cramped pews, spilling into the aisle.

There's a small stage out in front waiting for a performer. Next to the stage, the band plays a thigh-slapping version of "I never heard a man speak like this man before", and everybody is set into motion, converging in handclaps, shuffles, and hands to the sky. The house is in great voice and in even greater spirits.

"I ain't never heard a man speak like this before,
Never in my life, since I been born,
Oh, I ain't never heard a man speak like this before,
Never in my life, since I been born."

The public sing in harmony, while a young man in a crisp white shirt sets a microphone on the stage. A woman aged somewhere in her mid-forties and dressed in a forest green, steps awkwardly up to the mic and speaks.

"There are so many miracles in this church that it's hard to talk about one without talking about two or three others because they blend together to make a beautiful flow of miracles that changes our lives. I want to tell you about my story."

The crowd settles.

"I've got a job that I've had for a year, and it was got for me by a miracle," she continues. "A man employed me when I wasn't able to go to work for six weeks, and he waited for six weeks, with nobody working for him, because Pastor Gordon kept that job open for me."

The congregation applauds with a pitter-patter of hands, and all eyes stare like a galaxy at attention. The lady continues.

"I was one of the fortunate ones to visit Disneyland with this Temple. I was also doubly blessed on that trip to be sat in the company of our Pastor. In the course of our conversation, he asked me how I was doing in my job, and I told him that each month we were getting fewer and fewer orders and that my employers were going bankrupt, and that was all that was said. When we came back from the trip, my boss was in turmoil because the orders were pouring in so fast, he didn't know what to do with them."

Cries of "Hallelujah" ring out.

"My boss had to hire another woman, one of our fellow Temple members, full-time to keep up with the orders, and he still doesn't know what's going on. I didn't even think to ask for any help. It's just like the other day, and this might sound crazy to some outside these walls, but those people will never understand the power our pastor. Just the other day, I ran out of gas, and I had about a mile and a half to go to the service station and, well, my car just sputtered and stopped. I tried to start it and see if it would go a few more feet to save me walking when suddenly there was gasoline in the car. The meter went up a few notches, then down, then up a few notches, and up again, and I was able to get to the service station. I drove to the wrong side of the pump and had to circle around, I was so excited, and I had plenty of gas to do all this, and I didn't even ask for it.

The congregation applauds.

"And for thirty years I prayed to God, getting down on my knees, pleading and crying for help, and I got nothing but disappointment and heartache. And now we have a Pastor who loves each and every one of us so much that we don't even have to ask – the blessings simply appear. He wants to give us so much, everything we need and everything we desire and everything that's good appears to us, even before we ask."

The crowd rises and whoops. The speaker lifts her palms to the ceiling.

"How thankful we are, Pastor, thank you! With our Pastor here, I know everything is going to be all right. I just *know it!*"

With her last exultation, the crowd roars with delight, but she's not done.

"So, you know, Pastor, I'm going to come every single week, and if I can't come for any reason, I'm going to call you and let you know why!" Her expression transforms from grace to imputation, and she fixes it on the audience. The clapping and yelling sustains and then fades.

She departs the stage as the band picks up the energy with a smooth, soulful gospel number. People jump and sing. Halfway through the first verse, Pastor Quincy Gordon emerges on the stage.

The Pastor stands at the lectern and adds his voice to the song via the loudspeakers. His is a deep and commanding voice, and his posture is its equal; tall, upright, and broad. His hair is slicked back, and a long black shimmering gown falls from his shoulders down to his feet, as he moves, the material appears to flow like water. He raises a fist into the air, and his large gold watch glitters in the light. He lowers his hand slowly, deliberately. The watch's face blinks white as he takes it off. Extending out his arm, he offers it to a parishioner in the front row. The gift is accepted with delight.

The band settles into a softer melody, and the pastor speaks over the music with his clear diction and warm southern baritone.

"We come together today to build a better world. No more chains should bind us. Arise ye enslaved people, once and for all. The earth shall rise on new foundations. We have been naught, but we shall be all. We want no condescending saviors to rule us from their judgment hall."

The music fades, and the sermon begins with tranquil words.

"Now, each of you give a fond embrace and a salutary kiss of greeting to your neighbor. Let's fill this atmosphere with warmth and love."

Oscar hugs his mother, and more open arms surround him. People turn toward one another with open hearts. The Pastor embraces the man next to him and blows a kiss to the front row.

"Love is a healing remedy,' he says. "Freedom is faith. Let us believe. Let us be free." A sudden snap of confusion contorts the Pastor's face. He lifts a hand to his brow in apparent discomfort.

"Sister, Sister Barbara," he says. His discomfort dissolves into curiosity, and he looks out to the crowd.

"Sister Barbara. You're concerned about the loss of your sight? You're not able to see me clearly?"

An elderly woman rises to her feet. She stands hunched and unsteady in a canvas-colored smock. A pair of thick glasses cover her eyes. The pastor speaks to her.

"Things are just a blur to you, aren't they? You've had to stumble around recently, through crowds and you're not able to see people's faces clearly, even close up, are you?"

Sister Barbara lifts a tissue to her nose and takes a sharp breath.

"It's true," she says.

"You have told me nothing about your condition?"

"No, I haven't."

"Please, now." He strikes a pose, one hand on the podium, the other on his hip, his chin high in the air. "Take off your glasses, Sister Barbara. Let's just dare our faith tonight."

The woman is tearful. She removes her glasses and blinks at the Pastor.

"Look at my face," he says, slowly running his hands through the air around his head, turning her focus towards his eyes.

"I'm going to hold up some fingers for you. I want you to concentrate hard. Remember, I love you. The people love you. Now tell me, how many fingers do you see?" He reaches out a hand and gestures a number. Sister Barbara squints across the room.

"…Three…"

The room explodes. Tears run down Sister Barbara's face.

"You don't even need your glasses, child!" the Pastor looks triumphant. Sister Barbara weeps. "Let us all be thankful with her and feel her joy." The crowd gathers even more spirit.

"Little Miss Rosie Porter." The pastor's tone is sharp. He peers down at a little girl in the crowd, "I see you frowning down there. Why do you frown at me? Just because you are small in size and age doesn't mean you can hide from Father's gaze. Why don't you smile at me?"

"I do, sir," the nine-year-old says.

"Lies! The child lies. Even Sister Barbara, before she was healed, even with her bad eyes she could see you frowning. Let me tell you, Miss Rosie Porter, the sooner you let love into your heart, the better your life is going to be, little darling. So, get wise to it."

There's a flutter of applause. Little Miss Rosie Porter bows her head. The Pastor resumes.

"This administration serves no other purpose than to show mankind the road to love and freedom. Condescending saviors can stay in their judgment hall. I am here as an example to show you that with love and freedom you can bring yourself up with your own bootstraps, and you can become your own God. Not in condescension, but in resurrection and upliftment from whatever health condition, economic injustice or servitude you might have had to endure. Within you are the keys to deliverance. Within you is love and freedom. I have come to show you the only God you need is in you!"

A current of power charges the room and it jolts people into the air as the organ plays celebratory notes. Some people claw at their clothes, some screw up their faces, others tremor, hop and scream. Voices fight for dominance of both volume and gratitude. The Pastor continues in full throat.

"That is my only purpose in being here! When the transition comes, the soul of every man and woman will open like a flower, and there shall be no need for Gods or any other ideology, rituals, or traditions. There will be no concerns about tomorrow because every day will be Heaven. We will build the Heaven that man has dreamed about. We will have Heaven, but not the one taught to us by the rich – the one in which maybe one day we would be given a job shining shoes in the throne room! No. We'll have our own Heaven, here and now!"

The Pastor drives each word as if it were a nail. He stands like marble as the applause rises and falls.

"I want you all to know that I see you — I see your pain. These are the days when the American house is on fire, and we need to get on our way to protection. The fat cats will not look out for you. When America faces a crisis, the people with the greatest social and economic problems are the ones that are going to go first." The Pastor clicks his fingers.

"This morning, I heard the radio raving about a tremendous rainfall of such magnitude that the entire nation is fearful. That rain shows you two things – that God is on our side and that it is beautiful."

The crowd roars.

"A great storm is upon us. A cleansing rain is about to come down, and even Noah couldn't build an ark quickly enough for this one, but dear friends, dear loved ones, how I am good to you. I have found a place for us, a place of perfect sanctuary where you will be safe, you will be dry, and you will have all the supplies you need to live in freedom. Come five o'clock tomorrow evening, we'll get on our Greyhound buses, and we'll take all we can — men, women, and children — I will deliver safe passage to all!"

8

DOUBLE UP OR QUIT

Stephen's big California welcome is a cold bottle of Corkies beer at the legendary Rainbow Bar and Grill on Sunset Boulevard. It's dark inside and the bar's illuminated more by rope lights and TV sets than any other source. The walls and floors are painted matt black and pink and yellow posters are dotted here and there, advertising upcoming performances from local bands.

Although there are no smokers in sight, the musk of tobacco is ingrained in the interior. The sound of a distorted guitar cuts the air, and colorful gumball machines crowd a small seating area dominated by bar stools with Jack's black and white "Old No7 brand". Bottles of liquor huddle together on a long shelf behind the small, unmanned bar.

Two regulars keep an eye on things from the vantage of barstools close by the cash register. To their right sits a lonely video-gambling machine that the rock star Lemmy used to play all night and all day, as the legend goes.

"Eight-thirty," one elderly barfly says to another. "Any minute now."

The old boys sit and watch the TV news with glass in hand. A few other people start flowing into the bar from the restaurant down the hallway.

"What's on?" Stephen asks a passing woman.

"The President's address."

The room fills with people jostling for position, all trying to get a look at the TV above the bar. The air is tense, and Stephen wonders if war is about to be declared.

At eight thirty, the news fades out, the President of the United States fades in, centered on the screen, his hands clasped and resting on a large oak desk. The Stars and Stripes hang behind his right shoulder, the blue presidential flag at his left. He looks into the camera.

"My fellow Americans. Today the World Weather Organization has officially declared Hurricane Jason a category five hurricane. We've been in frequent contact with our citizens and officials on the west coast of our great nation. The hurricane is looming over the Pacific Ocean, and it's heading directly for California much quicker than anticipated. Time is of the essence. We are marshalling the full power of the federal government and the private sector to come to the aid of the American people. This is the most aggressive storm that any nation has faced in modern history, and one hundred million people lie in its path. I am here to give you the grave news that catastrophic damage will occur. We need to act now to save as many lives as possible.

"After consulting our top analysts and our military, I have decided to take several strong but necessary actions to protect American lives. We will be suspending all travel to California for the next ninety days. The new rules will come into effect immediately. To all those planning trips to the state of California, do not travel. These restrictions will be adjusted subject to conditions on the ground as and when they improve.

"California has officially moved into a state of emergency, and it is with urgency that I call for a complete evacuation of the state. This situation is unique in our history. Never before have we such an immediate threat to human life on our shores. As we speak, our fine military is mobilizing to assist us in our hour of need. Through an evacuation, we can greatly reduce the threat to our citizens, and we will ultimately support those in need throughout the hurricane and its aftermath. As our country braces for impact, I urge you to stay calm and begin the evacuation in an orderly fashion. I repeat, begin the evacuation in an *orderly* manner. We are opening up stadiums, churches, and city halls as gathering places for those who require assistance.

"No nation is more prepared or more resilient than the United States. As history has proven, Americans rise to a challenge, and we're all in this together. God bless you and may God bless America."

The President fades out. The bar is silent and many look at the screen in disbelief.

"Well, junior, drink up," says one old bar fly to another. With a slug of his drink, he grabs his coat and moves towards the exit, triggering an exodus.

"Screw this weather," Stephen says to them. "Sun always shines in LA, my ass. I'm staying right here and finishing my drink. No rain or damn President is going to tell me what to do,"

The bar is quickly empty, and his eyes settle on the video-gambling machine.

"Cheers, Lemmy. Looks like it's just you and me now, an honor to meet you'. Nobody I'd rather be in a hurricane with. And we might as well help ourselves to another beer. I think we deserve one for the road."

After several beers and almost a day later, Stephen wakes up in the driver's seat of his pickup with the sound of driving rain. His windows are smeared by a wash of water from a bright blinking sky. Desperately hungover, he looks at his phone and sees a message from Larry. It's a picture of a goofy looking kid with a stupid smile and the words, "Went to LA for the first time – Hurricane Jason".

"Oh, shit!" He rubs his face and, with a deep breath, starts the pickup and hits the gas. Destination: anywhere but here.

9

WE'LL BE RIGHT BACK…

Hazel is typically called to appear before the media when a scientific voice is required to counterpoint political rhetoric, and this evening's radio interview is no different. The studio's walls are black foam and there's a spongey yellow microphone in front of her. She peeks over it and listens to candidate for Governor, Patricia Bigham, make her case:

"Recession *is* inevitable. You can't have an entire state wiped out and assume everything is going to be fine for the rest of the country. And this is not just an American problem. Hurricane Jason will have global economic implications. The President had early warnings about this hurricane, and what did he do to prepare the state? Nothing. Congress will need to bail out California to the tune of $1 trillion, and the effects will ripple across the US economy for decades. And it's all due to a lack of preparedness on the federal level."

The host sits at a bright control board dotted with colored LEDs. He swigs cold black coffee from a stained mug, gulping before speaking.

"Patricia, you're getting *way* ahead of yourself here, and what you're doing is irresponsible scaremongering. Frankly, only the Democrats would politicize the weather. Now isn't the time for politics. The response to any disaster should be nonpartisan – but we all know that this whole situation is a hoax, a smokescreen that's been designed by the dishonest, do-nothing, deep-state Democrats to undermine the President. When will they stop trying to derail this country?"

The host puts his lips to the microphone. "And for those tuning in, you are listening to Hurricane Jason *Live* on KBBLBBL. We'll be right back after this."

"What the hell was that, Vance!" Patricia says.

The producer's voice comes through Hazel's headphones. "Look, I'm pretty sure the transmission is getting lost in the hurricane, so we might as well wrap this up and get out of here. I'll bring it back and we'll sign off. We're live in three, two, one."

"You're right back here with Vance Trick on KBBLBBL. I'm sorry, listeners, we're going to call this off early, but before we do, we have scientist Hazel Cox in the studio to explain a little about the realities of the hurricane. Hazel, controversially, you're of the opinion that the hurricane is nothing that California hasn't experienced before?"

In truth, the newest data shows that Hurricane Jason is growing rapidly, quicker than even Hazel anticipated. She composes herself.

"We've seen it before, but not since the 1930s, and I wouldn't call it a hoax, certainly not. It's a serious weather front, and citizens should take every precaution. With this hurricane's lifecycle, we can expect winds over one hundred miles an hour and persistent rain, typical tropical cyclone conditions. It's dangerous, but it'll be over within two to three days. So, keep calm and either stay in a safe lockdown location or temporarily relocate. That's my advice. I've no idea why the hurricane is being talked up as the reaper coming to harvest. It—"

"Sorry, folks. We're officially off the air,' the producer says. 'The hurricane's coming in hot and heavy, and it's dampened our signal. Time to go home. Be safe."

"Nice job," Vance says, "Shame nobody heard it."

Hazel takes off her headphones and calls Flynn.

"Flynn, that was a disaster. And I'm glad I dressed up for that. I thought this was supposed to be a TV appearance." She stands and rearranges the waist of her pencil skirt. "*That* wasn't worth the thirty minutes I spent on hair and make-up."

"It's time to go to the safe house, Hazel.' Flynn's voice distorts, cuts in and out. 'You know the address, but I'll text it to you, just in case and you know the drill; follow the directions to the Staples Center. Any government worker that hasn't evacuated yet will be there waiting for transport."

"I'm passing on that. I'm going to go home to a shelter I've already prepared."

"Hazel, we've been through this – all government employees have been ordered to evacuate. Go to the Staples Centre – I'm not arguing. If your predictions are right, you'll be back home in three days. If you're wrong, you'll be in a safe, secure location. Hey, no questions."

"Yeah. No questions, Flynn. I'm not going. That's all there is to it."

Flynn sighs. "Look, this isn't me telling you this – it's a mandate from the top. I didn't want to do this, but the word from Washington is that if the state's chief meteorologist won't play ball, then there's no point in having a state chief meteorologist at all. People in the administration already think you're difficult, so go to the safe house or lose the entire department. It's your call, but if I were you, I'd get myself to the Staples Center immediately."

10

THANKS, BOBBY!

Drew's sitting at his desk on a chair that always causes him lower back pain. To his right is a stack of Imagine cassette tapes. Perched on the end of his desk is last Thursday's copy of *The Evening Star* from Bucharest, a Do Not Disturb sign from the Milana hotel in Sofia, various airline boarding passes, and four pairs of elaborate-looking headphones. His coffee mug, which has a picture of a Spitfire flying high above the green of England, sits by his laptop. He fills the mug with hot coffee from a silver cafetière and types on the black finger-worn keyboard, staring blankly at what he finds:

```
https://www.nationalGeoBlog.com/news/202
1/3/weatherhurricane-jason-liveupdates/
```

Tuesday, March 16th, 2021, 5 pm

A tropical depression has stabilized over the horizon. The weather system is about 350 miles west of California.

Wednesday, March 17th, 2021, 11 am

The hurricane has strengthened. Strong winds are blowing at around 40 miles an hour. It's considered to be no more than a typical tropical hurricane. It is officially named Jason and is 230 miles west of California.

Thursday, March 18th, 2021, 3 pm

After a few more hours, Jason has grown stronger and is now a hurricane. Winds are blowing 75 miles an hour. It is 30 miles off the coast of California and about to make landfall much quicker than expected.

6 pm: The eye of the hurricane is expected to come ashore within two hours. The hurricane winds are 98 miles an hour and rapidly strengthening.

Howling winds beat Drew's apartment. The tap, tap, tapping of the blossom trees against the window is loud and getting louder.

The branch crashes through the glass, glinting shards blow across Drew's desk. The branch reaches inside and claws at him. He picks up his phone and makes a desperate video call.

"Come on! Pick it up!"

Bobby's smiling face appears on the screen in front of a snowy outdoor backdrop.

"Bobby! I need a plan!"

"What's up with you, lad?" Bobby's face glitches on the screen.

"The hurricane, it's bad! It's raining – a lot! And it's getting worse. I'm beginning to think the headlines weren't bullshit."

"There's no rain where I am, bud!" Bobby sniggers.

"Have you seen the weather reports? Where are you?"

"Colorado. Where are you?"

"Colorado! And what do you mean Where am I? Some manager you are…"

"Take a flight and come here. You'd love it."

"I can't take a flight! They've all been grounded!"

"Ah, you're screwed then."

"Yes, Bobby. I know I'm screwed. Thank you. Could you not have mentioned this on the plane? 'Drew, by the way, California is about to get nailed. You might want to think about leaving'."

"I did!" exclaims Bobby.

"No, you didn't! You're a twat…"

"Hey! You need to stop drinking, pal. Plus, it can't be all that bad. Just settle in. You're the one who insisted on living in LA in the first place."

"Stop laughing! My hangover's killing me, and the parking lot's flooding."

"What about that girl who lives over the way from you? The one you're always harping on about. What's she doing?"

"I don't harp on. I hardly mention her at all, but, yeah, the hot woman across the courtyard has gone. She's gone to someplace in the hills. I suppose if you're not going to help, I'll follow her."

"Good luck, Drew. I'll be thinking of you."

"Yeah. Screw you… What's that…? The connection's dropping. I can hardly see you. Wait, shut up, let me call you back and see if I can get a better line."

Drew redials. The call fails. He throws the phone at his bed, but remembering he paid $2,000 for the device, lunges to save it from crashing to the floor.

"Ah. Dammit! I suppose it's time to fire up the old wagon."

Tripping over his bags, Drew heads to his car with an armful of hastily seized essentials: a crate of cider, a bottle of gin, a two-foot-tall microphone, his watch, a change of clothes, a phone charger, and his laptop. He opens his apartment door and prepares to brave the elements.

He runs across the lot, through the downpour and scattering pink blossoms, to his relic of a Buick. He's soaked to the bone by the time he gets inside. He dumps his belongings in the back seats and starts the car. The engine howls and headlights stutter to life.

He sets a broad course for the hills as the wind whistles over the bodywork and the tires cut through a foot of water from the tidal surges.

"I don't have enough booze for this," he says, cracking open a can of cider.

The wipers brush away sheets of water and the Buick proves weatherproof enough. Water leaks from the window seals, and the air conditioning has stopped blowing. But who needs it? Drew reasons. "Come on, car, you sound like you're about to crap out a transmission, but you're doing fine."

Driving slowly on, he enters downtown California. There isn't a soul in sight, and every street is washed and deserted. The car is flanked by stores boarded up with plywood sheets. The tick of the car's turn signal is the only counterpoint to the rain. The gray skies grow charcoal black as the earth shakes in the hurricane's shadow and rallies of thunder warn the world underneath.

An alarm starts in the distance, slow and rhythmic, like the sound of an old air raid siren. It's joined by various other alarms in discordant syncopation. Rapid winds chime far-off church bells. Trash cans, plants, bicycles, and all manner of street debris rise and move in the air as if the world has been turned sideways. There's a loud crack close by, and the green head of a palm tree rolls across the intersection. Drew hits the brakes.

"What was that?"

An apparition outside – no, not an apparition, an actual person, walking the streets alone in these conditions. He can't believe it. He strains to see across the street with rain flowing thick over his windshield.

A tall figure dressed in black moves on the corner of St Vicente and 14th. The stop lights flex in the wind, a mailbox clatters and shimmies on its moorings, and, with no coat or any other defense against the elements, there stands a woman, looking every like damned ghoul – like a soul fated to perform some immortal duty on the deck of a sinking ship. The moment is long enough for Drew to realize the cold. In the gloomy sky, a dark rainbow appears. He winds down his window and appeals to the woman the only way he knows how.

"Hey! You friggin' idiot. What are you doing?" Rain pours over his face, down his neck, and into the car.

No response.

"For Pete's sake!" He rolls the window up, throws the car door open and runs to the woman. The weight of the downpour is ferocious. Within seconds, he feels like he's just walked out of a river.

"Are you OK?"

Her eyes are like ash flakes in bright crystal, and she stares right through him. He tries to seize her attention.

"You're *not* OK. I can tell. Listen, love, why don't you come with me. I know I'm a stranger in a strange car, but if you need a lift or someplace to go, you can come with me. You can't stay here – the rain isn't going to stop. You'll die out here."

She doesn't move.

"You can't die out here. It's too wet! Over there, that's my car. Let's get in, together. Come with me." He takes her by the wrist. "I know times are hard, believe me, I know, but let's get in the car and go somewhere safe, OK?"

She looks into Drew's eyes as water pours off her chin.

She moves with him as they hurry to the car.

"Phew!" he says, slamming the door. "Feels more like a bloody submarine in here! What's your name?"

Not even a glance in his direction.

"I know a place you can ride out the hurricane. It's on this map, look," he says.

She looks out of her window, her black dress sodden, her hair dripping.

"Ok fine. Anyway, my name's Drew, the last of a dying breed, but that might be a good thing. Nice to meet you."

The threat outside begins to consume the car. Drew reaches back and grabs another can of cider.

"Here's to your health, my dear. Wow, you see that?"

A vending machine, billowing black smoke, is being swept down the flooded intersection.

"That looks like I feel," Drew says.

The woman's stare extends well beyond the horizon, a horizon that's shattered by a jagged blue-white scar and the noise of a cracking whip. Downed overhead telephone lines whip the ground as the hurricane gains momentum and the bruised sky transforms into a censure on the lands. The darkness stretches rapidly across all that can be seen, and within minutes of touching land, the hurricane has brought a crisis. This kin of Jupiter has become the most powerful feature on earth, as if the planet rolls along its axis now. It draws a mighty breath.

God. Bless. America.

11

THE WORST IS YET TO COME

Hurricane Jason is yet to reach its peak, and as Hazel makes her way through California's darkening streets, she knows it.

She used to love the sound of heavy rainfall, especially on camping trips when the sound of pitter-patter on tent canvas would soothe her during the nighttime storms. And when the rain became heavy, it was even a little exciting to feel the power of nature rock the tent. But this rain is different. It strikes her car like white noise and threatens to trap her on the drenched, deserted streets.

Thunder cracks and the water rises. The front of her car parts the water like the prow of a boat, and with a jolt, the steering wheel spins out of her hands. She pulls the car back under control, but there's a watery thump coming from the passenger-side front.

Damnit!

She drives on. She only needs to make a one-way trip to the safe house, and everything else can be figured out later, but the thumping gives way to grinding, and the car comes to a halt. She steps into the rain and dashes to the front of the car.

A tire's blown out.

She throws herself back in the driver's seat, soaked to the bone, and reaches for her cell.

"Come on, Flynn. Come on! Pick up!"

Not even a dial tone.

She tries a breakdown recovery service. She tries 911, again and again – nothing. She tries Flynn one more time. She gets his voicemail.

"Flynn! Call me! I've had a blowout on Selma Avenue. I'm stuck in the hurricane. You need to call me back as soon as you get this. I need you to come and get me. I'm going to have to try and change the tire, but you gotta get out here."

The temperature drops and panic overtakes her frustration. It's half-light outside, and visibility is reduced to a close blur. She takes a breath and opens the door, shielding her face from the rain. She finds a tire iron and a jack in the trunk, and after a struggle with the spare, she kneels by the busted wheel and gets to work.

The lug won't turn.

"This is impossible!"

She puts her whole body weight behind the tire iron.

"Come on!"

It slips out of her hands and she falls against the car.

"This is hopeless!"

Her hands are raw, the road surface cuts her knees, and a steady stream of rainwater drenches her to her thighs. The black pencil skirt she wore for the studio isn't helping either. The downpour makes it impossible to change this tire, especially for someone more familiar with tropical cyclones than with auto repair.

The sky continues to fall, and she starts to feel like she's drowning. Panic swells. The bitter cold sets in and she curses herself for not bringing even the most basic emergency supplies. In a flash of adrenaline, her breathing becomes labored and she can hear her pulse. Reality sinks in, and she's not sure of anything anymore. Time slows. The noise of the rain is dulled, and her mind begins to wonder what shape death might take and what trauma she'll have to endure on this patch of wet road in downtown California.

Her vision is fuzzy. A large shape beckons her and speaks.

"Ma'am," a masculine voice calls out. Wet to her bones, she doesn't hear the voice clearly the first time.

"Ma'am!" the voice booms again. Time resumes, and so does the sound of the rain. A hooded man with an outstretched hand reaches for her.

"Come with me."

She tries to speak, but the wind blows away her words. She takes the hand, and they hurry across the road through the pacing rain towards a line of six silver buses. Their heavy diesel engines tick over, pelting raindrops sparkle through the headlights. The doors of the leader bus open – the driver is a heavily tattooed man. He waves them inside.

The bus is packed with people, and they cheer when Hazel appears. It's warm, and the bus feels sturdy against the elements. Hazel's savior lifts his hood and reveals a pastor's collar. He reaches for a microphone and addresses the people.

"Bless our beautiful Greyhound bus, this silver beacon of light and hope! We have another spirit to whom we can offer salvation to and save from a watery damnation. I said I would offer safe passage to all those who deserve it. I will take those who are worthy. By my almighty vision, I saw a woman in need. Hazel Cox, I knew your time would come. Please, take a seat with your brothers and sisters. Mother, offer Hazel a towel, a warm blanket, some coffee, some food."

An older woman smiles and puts a towel around Hazel. "Don't worry, dear, you're all right now," she says. "Oscar, fetch some coffee for Hazel. Bless you. You're so wet."

Hazel's grateful for the towel, not least because she's become acutely aware that the rain has rendered her white blouse almost see-through.

"How do you know my name?"

"My child, everyone in California knows Hazel Cox, the famous meteorologist. I've seen you on TV, and I've heard you on the radio many times these last few years."

She blushes from the recognition. "And what's your name?"

"You can call her Mother," interposes the Pastor, "She's my wife."

"Well, Mother, I need to get to the Staples Center. It's not far from here and I'd be grateful if you would drop me off."

"I'm afraid we can't take you there," the Pastor says. "It would be a mistake to go to the Staples Center on an occasion like this. Besides, I have my flock here, and it is my duty and honor to take these fine people to higher ground, to a safe place where they will be protected from nature's wrath. I offer you a place on our modest ark, Hazel. The hurricane makes our time limited. Please, come with us, come with us now. We can't leave you out in the storm."

"Thank you, but I really need to get to the Staples Center. It's a covered stadium that's being used as a pre-evacuation safe house for government employees. I'm expected there, and if I don't show up, my boss–"

"Hazel, Hazel, Hazel, be calm. There's no need to worry. Fate has brought us together and I will keep you safe. Here's a plan, why don't we mosey on to my shelter, and when we arrive there, you're more than welcome to contact your safe house, and if they're able, they can come by and pick you up. Do we have a deal?"

"I'm not sure I have a choice, so..."

"We always have a choice, Hazel. We always do, but I'm sure you don't want to go back out in the rain right now. We must press on. The worst is yet to come."

She takes a seat next to a young woman and is swarmed by well wishes. Someone hands her a blanket and coffee from a Thermos. At the back, she notices a row of stern, unflinching faces that carry a weight around their eyes. They sit motionless while the rest clap, sing, and cheer.

The woman at her side is heavily pregnant, no older than nineteen.

"Where are we going?" Hazel asks.

The young woman smiles as a tip of lightning explodes outside.

"We're going to Salvation."

12

IF YOU DON'T KNOW WHERE YOU'RE GOING, ANY ROAD WILL TAKE YOU THERE

After miles of wading through waterlogged roads, Stephen slows his pickup. The sky booms. He looks to his phone just as the screen cuts out. He launches it into the back seats and drives on, hoping to stumble across a plan. The elements howl against his pickup, shunting it from side to side. He scans the radio stations, hoping to find some information or any sign of life. He turns the black dial and watches the radio's red marker slide up the plastic scale. Nothing but static. The woolly, shifting noise from the speakers syncopates against the rainfall on the roof, giving the moment an unnatural feel.

He punches the steering wheel. "Oh Lord, I'm hungover as hell and I need a place to go. If there were ever a time to give me a sign, it'd be now."

He spies a curious hand-painted sign tied to a post at the next junction. It reads, "Salvation this way", and there's an arrow pointing left.

"God, you picked a fine time to be literal. Here I come, Jesus!" He slaps his hands. "Come on, Red. This calls for music, very loud music!"

He reaches to his glove box and fumbles around through a litter of long-forgotten items: an old parking ticket, a grubby cleaning cloth, and some deodorant. His determined groping continues until, "Ahhh…" all the answers are found, and he slips a well-worn AC/DC 8-track cartridge into the player. Suddenly life is better, living easy, living free, season ticket on a one-way ride. He shifts into drive and makes his way towards the most welcome, if not crude, sign.

The sign comes and goes, but moving along, he finds another, and another and another, all directing him to "Salvation". The signs are not so close together that he feels confident he will see another, but sure enough, mile after wet mile, the signs keep coming.

The sky darkens, the music runs out, and he feels he must be close to whatever Salvation is. The clouds crack and a brilliant blue flash fills the sky. Cold, watery winds rock his pickup, but the flooded roads are no match for trusty Red. Even as the tarmac gives way to a steep, winding dirt road, the pickup plows on.

Turning a bend in the road, the lights of his pickup shine on a rain-soaked, wind-blown concrete structure sheltering between high, wet tree trunks and flapping leaves. It looks abandoned but well-built, with coarse weather-beaten, mossy-green walls and an unsettling, angular shape.

"Looks like a bunker," Stephen mutters in an attempt to mute his rising anxiety. The building gives the surroundings a mystical, almost supernatural atmosphere.

The sky canon booms again and white lights strobe.

Why would someone put so much concrete in the middle of the woods?

The bunker stares back at him. It's an engineering feat but rough-looking with the aura of something sinister. He wonders what its purpose is. *Perhaps military? Likely military.* Its very existence seems to signal conflict. Looking down on California from the hills, its intriguing time-worn exterior suggests it once had some dark, definite purpose. But now it feels like an island, like whoever designed it wanted the inhabitants to feel they're on the edge of the world. He ventures outside for a closer look.

The temperature has plummeted, and the rain sweeps through at shifting angles as he approaches the building. The ruin has a haunting beauty, but it's a decaying shell. There are no windows and there's only one door. A sign hangs above it: "Welcome to Salvation".

A car engine whines in the distance, coming closer.

This could be good news. Misery loves company, after all.

He steps out of the doorway.

A crack of thunder breaks the night, and the rain falls like an ocean. Stephen gets bogged down in the thick mud, and his feet sink in a mire. Using both hands to pull his feet out of the mud, he's illuminated by the headlights of a speeding, meandering car that's started to slalom and buck in the deep wet ground.

The car doesn't stop. The impact is swift and horrible.

The windshield smashes as Stephen bounces over the car.

"What was that!" Drew shouts. "A deer? This damn rain! I can't see shit!"

He leaps out and races to the rear, hoping, praying he didn't just kill someone. Lit by the Buick's lights, he finds Stephen's crumpled figure, his face smeared with mud and blood.

Drew suddenly feels slow and drunk. He kneels beside Stephen.

"Don't die! Please don't die. Somebody, help!"

Dazzling white lights approach, and with a screech of breaks a bus appears.

"Pick that man up out of the mud." commands an emphatic southern voice, clear enough to cut through the wind and rain. "Get the doors of our sanctuary open so that Salvation can be this man's place of healing. Quickly, there's no time! Can't you see both his legs are broken? Broken clean in half! Get the stretcher from the medical bay."

The driver leaps out of his seat and runs to the door of the bunker, heaving open the large steel door. Several men follow him inside.

"My boots, I need my boots. They got stuck in the mud." Stephen whispers. "And my legs aren't broken, look…" Before another word can leave his mouth, the driver returns with a gurney and three other people. They lift him onto the stretcher, and he's carried into the mouth of the monolith.

13

IN THE SHELTER OF EACH OTHER, THE PEOPLE LIVE

All six buses spill their passengers into the mud and the rain as the Pastor leads his three hundred into the dark of Salvation's entrance corridor.

"Is everybody inside?" he yells.

"I think so," comes the response.

The door slams closed, trapping the hurricane outside and plunging the corridor into darkness. With a thunk and a whirl, a generator blinks dim lights into life, and the drenched figures trudge deeper into the shelter.

The air is damp. Green stains grow up the walls, around the door and mix with the shadows. Hazel follows the crowd through the musty walkway into an open space, where pews and a lectern are waiting.

A huddle forms at a table stacked with towels. The Pastor takes one, dries his hair by the lectern and asks the people to take a seat. Hazel looks around for the injured man, but he's nowhere to be seen.

"Good evening, ladies and gentlemen. I'm so glad you're all here," the Pastor begins. His greeting sets off cheers, laughter, and general relief as people stagger along the pews. They shuffle and bunch to make space. Every inch of every pew is taken.

"Welcome to Salvation!" the Pastor says, with both arms spread wide. The congregation break into steady applause.

"I know all of you are ready for food and for your beds, so this will be a quick meeting to orientate you. We've had one hell of a day, I know. I've never known a day like it. It's been a very special day. After this meeting, everybody, get some rest or enjoy some evening entertainment. We'll have music and dancing in the Common Room. It's just a little down the corridor, by the kitchen, further on up to the left.

"And each of you should look forward to breakfast tomorrow, a hearty breakfast, be ready for that. The Planning Committee will get you up at seven. There are things to be done here if this is to be a home for us all. Let us all be grateful for this shelter and its mighty walls. That hurricane is going to be with us for quite some time. Many people have escaped the State, but many more did not find transport or shelter, and that's a tragedy, but we have our ark, and its mighty door and its mighty lock, so let us be thankful."

The crowd agrees. The Pastor continues.

"We are all illuminated by electricity created by the many generators we purchased with our sweat and blood, and they will give us power for everything we need. We have a special loudspeaker system, a public address system, so I can talk to you all and make announcements into every room throughout the day, so you'll be kept informed. You'll miss nothing.

"We have all the supplies we need. We have coffee, cans of fruits, all kinds of fruits. You wouldn't believe it. We have Mylo – an extremely good drink, cheddar cheese, evaporated milk, boxes and boxes full of supplies. We have beds, mattresses, sheets. We have tremendous supplies built up by our workers – every vegetable every kind of delicious food. We have rooms and rooms of supplies and medications. We have manuals, we can do surgery if we have to. We have all sorts of books on every procedure – technical books on how to build anything we need and maintain everything we have. We have a drug we've found that's supposed to not only stop cancer but reverse cancer – what's it called? Cornella? Yes, Cornella. And those working in the kitchen will bake it into all the food we eat. You may notice the taste. When used on meat, it makes a rare roast, a beautiful roast. You've never tasted a roast like it. We have a refrigerator, a beautiful walk-in freezer to store our food; we have sinks, and a big, big cooking stove – many people would love a stove like this. We will be comfortable. We have modern furniture, most of it made by our brothers and sisters, all beautifully handmade. We have clothes we can tailor to suit you, and we have showers and facilities enough for all."

The list stops. Pastor Gordon looks at the open Bible on his lectern.

"You must all feel like I feel. Let us all be thankful." He speaks slowly. His followers are committed to every word. From the edge of their seat, they lean forward, but not everybody is so attentive.

Hazel runs a towel over her head and observes the room. There's a level of dusty decadence and crooked luxury to the space. In years gone by, someone had clearly poured money into it. The interior is well-appointed, which surprises her. She expected to see nothing but dank gray walls, but instead she finds a well-maintained open space. An old-looking piano sits in the corner, waiting to be played. Modern loudspeakers are an ugly recent addition. Between the loudspeakers and from a simple wooden lectern, Pastor Gordon stands, still wearing his long but very wet black gown. He speaks, but Hazel isn't listening.

Just be polite, she tells herself. It's shelter for now. It's too dangerous to go anywhere tonight anyway.

She looks at the faces around her. What a random collection of people.

She looks at her phone and sighs. Zero signal.

"We have some new faces with us," the Pastor says, "some new family members to complete our perfect jigsaw of personalities. I'm pleased to announce that Hazel Cox is one of them."

Hazel's eyes snap up from her phone.

"How fitting that a weather scientist joins us on our mission. There are other new faces you may notice, so let us all welcome them to our collective bosom. You know, earlier, Hazel told me that she had plans to take shelter at the Staples Center."

The crowd laughs.

"We all know what happened in the Superdome in New Orleans when Katrina hit, don't we? My golly, those people inside were trapped for six days with no electricity, no water, the toilets stopped working, and even with the National Guard in there, the public were raping and killing each other, just tearing each other apart. How horrible, how horrible. It got so bad that the National Guard left them to it. Hazel, I'm glad I have spared you from that tonight, and I'm so thankful you're here with us."

The congregation applauds.

"There will be some things that Hazel and the new members will have to get used to. It will be an adjustment. Just to clear the slate – we say everything to everybody's face here. No criticism – you can't say anything behind anybody's back. If you do, you're in trouble. If you want to say something to the family, or to me, about me, that's fine. I welcome it. We grow stronger for it. Now, do you understand the essence of what I'm saying?"

Three hundred heads nod under wet towels.

"Of course, we also have the company of an unfortunate young man who was run down by a car outside Salvation's door. I will be visiting him in due time. Thank goodness for our medical supplies. As the west coast of America is washed away and while the ecosystem is getting all fucked up, we can sit here with a million dollars' worth of medical supplies. We could withstand a nuclear fallout, ladies and gentlemen. We have so many miracles.

"Speaking of miracles... I was thinking the other day about a few services back when a man came to me, and just to show you that there is nothing lost in this consciousness, brother Aiden, back there, you came to me, concerned about something that was lost?"

A man stands and nods.

"Aiden, you were concerned that you lost something miles and miles away. I can tell you that today my spirit retrieved it for you. Come and take it."

The Pastor produces a gold credit card from inside his gown. He taps it on the lectern and holds it in the air. As Aiden takes the card, people cry "Oh yeah", "Oh golly", and "Praise be."

"You see, nothing can be lost in this consciousness. Do you understand the mystery? Do you understand my power? I see all. I know all. Did you hear that? I *see* all. I *know* all. Let that sink in, and let me tell you this – if you don't need a God, I'm no harm to you."

Low yells of "Yeah" and "Preach" follow in the Pastor's vocal riptide.

"But if you do need a God, I, personally, will edge out your Sky God, no problem. Do you understand what I'm saying? Let me explain – does any other church have love? Those other preachers, did they deliver you to Salvation tonight? Do they have buses? Have they given you a home? Have they given you any help? Do they go into the court and the jail and set you free?"

"No!" shout many voices.

"What about Sky God? Did Sky God Jesus – did he do any of those things for you?"

The Pastor pounds the lectern.

"No! I'm the only one that will help you because I'm the only one who cares about you! I'm the only one that loves you! There is only one hope, only one glory, and that is me, your *father*. And to those in need of a Sky God I spit on ye bible and cast out its word."

He picks up the open Bible and lifts it high, demonstrating it to the crowd. His eyes bulge, his nostrils flare. He lowers the Bible to his chin and spits on the printed words with an exaggerated, emotionally suffused extravagance. The he launches the Bible down the aisle. It flies six feet and bounces along the floor.

The room gasps.

"You see! Nobody's going to come out of the sky!" he yells. "I did not get cast down by lightning bolts. I see that some of you are not aware of what God is. Let me educate you – God is perfect freedom, justice, equality, and love. There's only one thing that can bring perfect freedom, justice and equality and perfect love in all of its beauty – and that thing is me!"

"Hell yeah!" says one voice from the pews. Claps and yells spark from all quarters and a few stand with violent agreement. The Pastor's voice grows in power, his words fall like granite.

"I have come to make one final dissolution. One final elimination of all religions. And until I have eradicated them from the face of the earth, I shall do all the miracles that you said your God would do and never did. I shall come and heal you all of the diseases that you pray to be healed, but never are. You have also seen all the gifts and faculties of a woman who could not see and is now healed. All that I do is done to remove all the images of the condescending saviors that you have. All the symbols of the heavens, the judgment halls and the Sky God consciousness, I will eliminate them all from the opinions of people, so you recognize finally and completely that there is no Sky God!"

The Pastor lifts his hands, commanding the crowd to cheer, and they do so with pleasure, and the applause rings long. He goes on in full throat, distorting the loudspeakers. His delivery is rhythmic, almost hypnotic, and his fervor grows swollen and outrageous.

"It is written that ye are Gods – I'm a God and you're a God! So, I'm a God, and I'm going to stay a God until you recognize that you're a God – and when you recognize you're a God, I will disappear, but until then, I'm going to be very much what I am – God almighty God!"

The crowd is a wash of emphatic noise. The Pastor takes a breath but quickly strikes again.

"And I must say it is a great effort to be God, I would wish it upon another, but no one else has the faculty that I do. When they do, I shall gladly hold their coat, but until then, I am God. And I will have no other Gods before me. Beside me, there shall be no other. As my rage purifies the land outside these walls, I will keep you safe inside my Salvation, because I am God, and this is my Temple!"

He raises a fist and the crowd reach a frothing ecstasy.

Hazel starts to question her luck, and all the things it has brought her because now, at first reaction, luck is all she has to blame for this situation. The same force that, at other times, had spilled coffee down her blouse or stubbed her toe or forgot to set her morning alarm. After witnessing this sermon, it's now clear that not only had luck deserted her, but it actually hated her all along. She purses her lips and widens her eyes so much that she feels them almost turn into exclamation points. Looking up at the gray cobwebbed ceiling, she mutters the only words she can muster.

"What. The. Fuck."

14

THE FIRST IMPRESSION IS ALWAYS THE RIGHT ONE

The Common Room has none of the Sermon Hall's aged elegance, it is, however, bigger and set out with parallel rows of wooden tables and chairs made from the roughest, sturdiest looking timber. A band plays between two loudspeakers at the far end of the room. People stand, some play games and talk while others sit and listen.

An old man in a brown suit jacket and a charcoal flat cap runs his fingers over the keys of an electric piano, and the clean white china clinks and chimes in sympathy with his cheery mellow mood. A younger man creates a wash of rhythm on a small drum kit while a guitarist and a bass player fill the gaps.

"I'd like to introduce the lead singer of the band," says the old piano player, "Please welcome to the stage, eleven-year-old Miss Karis Fletcher."

You can't hear the outside world – no patter of rain, no boom of thunder, and no rushing of winds. In the dim light of the Common Room, you can almost imagine this little girl's voice has calmed the storm outside. She sings a version of "You Are So Beautiful" but replaces the words "You are" with the words "Salvation is".

Some listening wipe a tear from their cheeks, while a few men provide a counterpoint to the melody, thanks to a rough game of dominoes. They slap tiles onto the tabletop and haw at each other.

The room is warm, a little too warm, thanks to the heat escaping from a kitchen adjacent to the stage. A peek through the serving hatch shows a busy cook at work. The heat brings the smell of simmering food. Details of tonight's menu are pinned to the wall:

Tonight's meal will be rice, peas, and carrots.
One scoop per person.

People with plates in hand approach the sign and shake their head. Hazel hears the conversation between people at the serving hatch, "No meat tonight, the Pastor says so. Maybe tomorrow."

That's fine for Hazel. She's already decided she isn't hungry for the church's food, or its company. She's made no observance of the room aside from locating a faraway seat to occupy. She doesn't see the domino players slapping tiles on the tabletops, and she doesn't notice the open-mouthed laughter from the thick spectacled lady on the table opposite. She's unconscious to the sound of the singer's voice because she's preoccupied with two things: her phone and its lack of signal. She covers herself with a towel, the nails of her left hand tap the tabletop and mutters to herself. Anxiety twists inside her and the embers of a dreadful recognition begin to glow.

"You wouldn't believe the day I've had," says a voice from a seat opposite.

She bunches her shoulders and folds her arms.

The voice leans in. "My day, if you'll allow me, started this morning when I learned a big storm was coming towards America, and this hurricane, likely to cause large scale devastation, was pointing straight at me. I think I may have been the last person to hear the news. Then I met a woman, I think she's crazy, and I've no idea where she's gone." He rises from his chair and looks around the room. "Then I hit a man with my car, terrible thing that. Then I met a mad pastor, pastor? Is that the word? Pastor? Anyway, I met this mad pastor and watched him throw a book across a room, and now I'm here. So, that's my day so far, but the night is young, and there's still plenty of time to fuck it up. My name's Drew. You?"

"Hazel." She unfolds her arms. "I'll save you the time. You recognize me from TV."

"I don't watch TV, it's too much of a commitment." Drew yawns into his hand. "So, what are you in for?"

"I'm a meteorologist, and although I've known about the hurricane for weeks, I somehow ended up on the crazy bus with you people."

"Ha! Yeah, that's pretty stupid," says Drew. "At least I have ignorance as an excuse." He casts a quick eye over her sullen, soaked form. "So, some hurricane, huh?" He adds, "How about dinner?"

"What about it?"

"What about what?"

She sighs and looks at her phone.

"Hold on. What do you mean by 'you people'?" Drew says.

"No offense."

"Ah, the old 'no offense', eh? I guess I make a bad first impression. Let me start again. My name's Drew, I'm thirty-

75

two, a DJ, formerly of Liverpool, England. Is it ok if I sit with you for a while?"

Hazel's austerity relaxes into curiosity. "Sure, why not," she says, sliding her phone away. "So, Drew of Liverpool, England, you told me how you ended up here tonight, but how did you end up in California in the first place?"

"Now that's a story. I'll start at the beginning – first I was a DJ, then I moved to California – oh, I suppose that's the end. I thought that story was longer. Anyway, hopes and dreams brought me here, hopes and dreams, and other frivolities."

"That's an old story in this town, it's full of hopes and dreams, but they're not frivolities."

Drew narrows his eyes and teases a smile. "But that *is* what they are: frivolities, pure folly, old and young, for all races on earth. Hopes and dreams aren't good things. They keep you up at night, they make you worry, they make you ill."

"I suppose next you'll tell me that charity is for suckers, ambition is for losers, and love makes you nauseous."

"Nah. I've thought about love. I can't shake the idea that love is a marriage between hopes and dreams, and love is, in fact, nothing but a weapon. Think about it, if you were to look at all of humanity, all of its history, and place on one side of a scale all the good that love has done, and then on the other side place all the suffering that love has caused, you'd find a very uneven balance. Love is responsible for more human suffering than cancer and nuclear bombs combined, because they're all made worse by love."

Hazel turns away. "That's not a very churchy point of view."

"What?"

Hazel laughs.

Drew laughs. "Maybe my second impression isn't better than my first. Just choose the most flattering of the two."

She shakes her head. "Is everyone in this church like you?"

"I've no idea. You tell me."

"Oh! I'm not – I thought you were! So, you're not with these people?"

"No, but I did run one of them over," Drew says, waving a finger as if it counted for something.

"That's terrible."

"I do feel bad about it. I'm sure I do. I must check on him."

"Are you sure you're not crazy like these people?"

"What makes you think these people are crazy?"

"Did you hear that sermon earlier? Anyone who follows that guy must be a little, you know." She rolls her eyes and taps her head.

"Hey, Drew!" A voice calls from across the room. "You waste no time making new friends. You better make sure you tell Father!"

"What? Oh, hi." Drew stands up in a hurry. "You made it! Great. Hi, hi, hi. This here is Hazel. Hazel, meet Megan. Megan's my neighbor. Her house is being swept away as we speak, just like mine."

Megan shakes her head. "What a day!" She brightens. "You made it here in one piece. That's good."

"Is it?" Drew says.

"Of course, I'm glad you made it here. But I wasn't joking, Drew. In our church, when you meet someone special, you have to declare it to Father first otherwise people will talk, and someone will report you."

"I've literally just met this woman, and *report* me? I'm not in this church. What are you talking about?"

"I'm teasing but take it as an FYI that in this church, relationships have to be sanctioned to be seen as proper. I'm being selfish in bringing it up really. I only mention it because there's someone here I like, a lot."

"Oh, yeah?" Drew sputters.

"Yeah, he's right here."

"He is now?" interjects Hazel, seeing a flicker in Drew's eyes.

"Yes, he is. I've known him from afar for a while, and he's handsome, a little aloof, and I'm really into him, so tonight I asked Father to green-light our relationship so I can proceed."

"…And?" asks Drew.

"And… He gave me the go-ahead!"

"Congratulations, I'm sure you'll be very happy together," Hazel says.

"I think so too. So, Drew, if you would, I'd really like it if you would meet Huxley. Come here, Huxley."

As if from nowhere, Megan produces Huxley. "Isn't he handsome!" She wraps her arms around him.

He's a six-foot-tall clean-shaven man with a large profile and a thin neck. He stands at Megan's side with the blank-yet-mobile expression of a man who wants to say something but has no idea of what that thing is.

"Say hi, Huxley." Megan smiles.

"Hi."

Hazel smirks.

"Hi, Huxley…" Drew says, finally. "Boat much? You look like the sailing kind. Good weather for it? Ah, shit, sorry, I'm sobering up."

"Well, we gotta go and share the good news with everybody." Megan turns away. "I'll see you all later!" She finishes with a wave.

Still smirking, Hazel lets a full beat pass. "I guess love is a weapon."

"It bloody is. And, for the record, I didn't say I didn't like love, it's just, you know. What does she see in *that* guy? He looks like a bore, and he's got the biggest face I've ever seen on a man. And he has a moron's smile."

"That was great," Hazel says.

"What do you mean?"

"I don't think she likes you very much."

"What makes you say that?"

"That was a total burn–"

"Help!" The cry comes from across the room. It's followed by several shouts of "Lord! Oh, Lord!" and "Praise be!" from various places.

"Somebody else has heard the news then." Drew looks over at a commotion near the dance floor.

"I don't think it's that." Hazel springs to her feet. On the other side of the room a crowd is forming a cautious circle. Sitting in the middle, on the floor, is the dull-eyed, heavily pregnant teen Hazel sat next to on the bus.

"What's wrong?" Hazel runs over.

A film of sweat has formed on the pregnant woman's brow and through her tightly tensed jaw, she appeals.

"Help! I think my baby is coming!"

15

NEW LIFE

A crowd surrounds the pregnant teen.

"Stand back, give her some space!" Hazel pushes the people away. "Someone get towels, and warm water. Is there a doctor here? Or a nurse?"

A few people mumble.

"Nurse Chamberlin!" shouts the teen. "Somebody get Nurse Chamberlin!"

"Go! Get the nurse!" Hazel shouts to a confused-looking man, who, prompted by her sharp look and a shout of "Now!", dashes off. She turns her attention back to the girl.

"What's your name, honey?"

"My name is Easter," she whispers. Her stomach is heavy, she arches her back and groans.

"OK, Easter, I know this is painful and I know it's less than ideal but you're about to have a baby, so you need to open your legs. If it helps, all the men can leave, OK?"

Easter nods.

"OK, guys, you heard, leave," Hazel says. "Go on. Go!"

A line of men shuffles to the exit.

"No, no, not my Sid!" Easter's eyes rush with panic.

"Who's Sid? Where is he?"

"Sid is her husband, dear," the Pastor's wife says. "I sent him to get the water and towels."

She takes Easter's hand. "Easter, don't you worry, I'm here for you, and so are all the girls. Breathe for me. Your Sidney got us here, he drove us to Salvation and now you're going to have his baby in safety, thanks to him."

"Easter, you need to breathe, OK? Breathe!" Hazel and Mother inhale and exhale together. Voices of sympathy and encouragement speak over Hazel's shoulder. Easter spreads her legs, and her face is tense and pained. She cries out. The last few men pick up their pace towards the exit.

"Stay calm, you're very dilated," Hazel says, "so this isn't going to take long. Keep breathing and when I say *push*, you push, OK? Now – Push!"

The air is hot. As the child crowns, a collective gasp takes the air.

"Push!"

Easter's hair is mottled wet and flat against her forehead. Her face is red. She cries again.

"Push! You're nearly there, you're doing great, stay with me, Easter," Hazel says.

"Where's Sid?" Tears roll down Easter's face.

"He's on his way with towels and water. Stay with me now. Push!" Mother says.

Sid arrives, bringing towels and water. "Here I am, baby, here I am, here I am." Sid mops Easter's brow with a towel then takes her hand from Mother.

"Push!" Hazel says.

Easter grips his hand. Mother puts a towel between Easter's legs. Seconds or minutes pass. Tension eventually gives way to relief; pain gives way to exhaustion. A small, thin, throaty cry from new lungs pierces the air. A life is brought into the world and into Hazel's arms. She cleans the baby up as much as she can and wraps the little delicate form in a towel.

"It's a boy! He's beautiful!" Hazel says, close to tears. She hands the child to Easter and the new mother weeps as she holds the baby to her bosom and rocks to and fro.

"What do you think, Sid?" Easter whispers.

"He's perfect. Thank Father, he's perfect," Sid leans in for a kiss.

The Pastor walks into the room and parts the crowd. A woman in a nurse's uniform trails behind.

"Congratulations," he declares. "What a precious scene. Praise be. A new child, a miracle has happened for all of us. What a miracle, Easter. What a miracle."

"Thank you, Father. He has your eyes," Easter replies.

The nurse gathers up the baby and assures the new mother of its health.

Far across the room, sitting silently, is Drew's driving partner – the still-drenched woman in black. She observes the scene and is not moved, until Sid comes into view. In a skipped heartbeat, she recognizes the tattoos on his arms.

It can't be him. But it is…

She knows those tattoos. She could spot them anywhere. They're forever etched in her mind as belonging to the man who raided the supermarket and killed her husband. With a rush of thoughts and a swirl of emotion, her anger ignites.

He will feel my pain. He will pay for what he did to Ethan, and I will have my revenge. Revenge is all that's left. Not now, but soon…

16

NEVER ARGUE WITH A FOOL. AN ONLOOKER MAY NOT BE ABLE TO TELL THE DIFFERENCE

Some of the men who had evacuated the Common Room took refuge in the Sermon Hall, in an attempt to eavesdrop on the action next door.

"What's she going to call the baby, *Good Friday?*" Drew sniggers.

No one's listening.

"Ha, get it, Good Friday, right? 'Coz, you know, her name's *Easter?*"

"Shush!" Huxley says. "I can't hear a thing with you going on!"

A few of the men, including Huxley, have an ear pressed against the smooth concrete wall that adjoins the two rooms.

"I'm losing interest by the second," Drew says.

Hazel, Megan, and Mother walk in, laughing at the men awkwardly craning their necks.

"The party's over, guys," Megan announces. "Easter's in the medical bay. She's had a beautiful little boy."

"Megan, why didn't you tell me this place is nuts?" Drew says.

"Nuts? A woman just gave birth. Deal with it."

"I don't mean that – I mean the Pastor, he's a little on The Spectrum, don't you think? And all these followers. It's all a bit... you know?"

"No. I don't know. There's nothing wrong with this place if that's what you're trying to say."

"After an hour here, I dunno about that." Drew murmurs.

"Would you have preferred to stay out there in the hurricane? You ought to be grateful."

"I am, I think. But I don't understand your church. What do you believe in exactly? That Pastor?"

"At least we have something to believe in, unlike you."

"Look, I don't want a heavy argument about faith. Let's just get along, at least until this thing blows over."

"This *thing* will blow over when Father wants it to blow over." Megan clenches her fists. "Say *thank you*!"

"What?"

"I said, say thank you, you ungrateful asshole. I knew I shouldn't have given you directions here."

She steps up to Drew.

Mother stands between them. "Come on now, Megan, we'll go and clean up the Common Room. It's no good standing around here arguing. Let us go and be of use."

Megan takes Huxley by the arm and leads him out of the room.

Mother turns to Drew. "We'll have no trouble here."

He sighs.

"And bedtime is at ten," Mother looks between Hazel and Drew. "We don't allow mixed sex accommodation here. You'll be given lodgings accordingly."

"I don't want to lodge with him," Hazel says.

"Rude,' Drew shrugs.

"I'll be back to allocate you a room before ten," Mother walks off into the gloomy corridor.

"Wow, I need to get out of here," Hazel says, watching Mother leave.

"You and me both," Drew says, "but what can we do?"

She looks at her phone. Zero bars. "I don't know. We wouldn't last ten minutes outside in the hurricane. I need to call for help before my battery dies. I need to find some cell service around here."

"These walls are way too thick, plus the storm – you won't have any luck." Drew looks at his watch. Water floats over the dial. "Hmm, my knock-off Rolex died in the rain. And the tail has fallen off the 'R'. I guess it's a genuine Polex now."

Hazel checks her phone again, its bright light casts over her face. "It's already close to ten and I'm exhausted. Some rest will do me good. Let's talk with the pastor in the morning and explain our situation. He can't keep us locked up in here. Can he?"

Back in the Common Room the ladies find clean-up dirty work. Fluids pool in small thick puddles and smear the polished floor where Easter had given birth. Each person on the cleaning crew has a large yellow sponge and an orange bucket of soapy water.

Huxley and Megan get to their knees and scrub.

A microphonic whine rings from the loudspeaker on the wall. The Pastor clears his throat and speaks through the tinny PA system:

"I am very pleased to announce that our
thriving community has just grown by a
count of one tonight. Congratulations to
the new mother, Easter. She's given
birth to a beautiful boy. She and her
baby are currently in the medical bay,
resting. Well done. We all send our best
thoughts to you. Much love from
everyone. That is all."

"Look, I want to know every word that Drew says, OK?"
Megan says. "One false step and I'm going to ball his ass up
and feed it to Father. He has a reckoning coming, sooner or
later." She stretches out her scrubbing elbow and glances over
her shoulder. Nancy and Lou kneel close by, but it's ok, they're
both half deaf.

"…Urgh! This is disgusting," Huxley says, "I can't believe
you roped me into cleaning this." He looks at the stains and
screws up his face.

"Don't be a baby. It's natural, and somebody has to clean it
up. Think of poor Easter. She looked exhausted."

"So, what's your problem with that Drew guy, anyway?"

"I don't have a *problem.*" Megan throws her sponge at the
floor and scrubs. "He just thinks he's better than everyone else.
You must have seen the way he looks at everybody, like he's
too good for us. He's a lazy slob and a washed-up DJ. I should
have never told him about this place. I only did it because
Father encouraged us to bring in new people, but now he's here
I think he's trouble, so we need to keep a close eye on him."
She punches the sponge into the bucket.

―――――

17

TOM'S THUMB

"I'm sure you'll find this perfectly comfortable." Mother says, walking Drew into a small room. "It's lights out at eleven. Breakfast starts at 6 am.'

She leaves.

Drew walks a circle around the room - a small circle, as that's all the room can accommodate, and he observes every detail: the large speaker hanging on the wall between the beds; the single bulb and the dusty ceiling; and the garish orange patterned bed sheets. He tests the mattresses on both beds, the coarse timber frames of which echo the unsophisticated tables and chairs in the Common Room and were presumably cut and nailed together by the same man or woman on whose labor everybody in Salvation rests. During his second loop of the room – monitoring the lines and scuffs in the concrete floor – his vision comes upon two new features: a pair of sneakers.

He looks between the worn-out, flat-soled tennis shoes and he sees they're attached to two legs. Their owner is a teenager clutching a backpack.

"All right, son," Drew says.

The young man checks Drew over. A smirk twitches on his face.

"All right, Pops. My name's Tom."

"Good. My name's Drew." They nod, as if they had come to an understanding.

"Where you from?" Tom asks.

"Liverpool, England."

"I wondered what that accent was. I'm staying in this room too. Which bed do you want?"

"That one." Drew points at the bed at the far wall. "It's the furthest from the door. That'll do fine."

"Yeah, it's a good bed. I like it too." Tom represses a smirk.

"Oh, do you now?"

"Yeah. I tell you what, since I like that bed and you like that bed, there's only one thing we can do to decide who gets it – to make the choice fair, I mean."

"What are you on about? That bed's mine," Drew says.

"It seems to me that whenever a disagreement occurs between two people, when you have your side and I have mine, such as in this case, the only tried and true way to break the impasse is…"

"Is?" Drew hastens the point with a gesture of his hands.

"We have to wrestle for it."

"What?"

"We have to wrestle for it. It's the only way. It's best to settle disagreements with a fight immediately. I've always known that. It's quick and it's simple and there can be no arguments afterwards."

"You're mad. I've got a mad roommate, haven't I?"

Tom drops his bag. "Great, the first to submit wins the bed."

"Hold on. I've already crippled a man today and that's usually my limit. How about an arm wrestle instead?"

"But we don't have a table or a chair, or anything to rest our elbows on," Tom says, looking about. "You can't arm wrestle on a bed. Mattresses are too spongy."

"Sounds like you're scared."

"Nonsense. I'm up for anything, anytime, anywhere. I've never been scared. I've fought and won for everything I've got in life"

Drew points at the rucksack flopped on the floor by Tom's feet. "Looks like all you've got in life is that red bag."

"Ah, but what's in the bag?"

"I dunno…" Drew stares at it.

"My point is, I don't back down, and I'll prove it." Tom adopts the forward pose of a grappler.

"All right, but wrestling isn't going to happen, and neither is an arm wrestle, apparently. So now what?" Drew says.

"Fair, fair." Tom relaxes. "I'll tell you what we'll do. But I'll warn you - it's what I do best, it's what I do better than anybody in the world."

"Righto, son. What is it?"

"Thumb war."

"Thumb war?"

"Yes, thumb war!"

"You mad bastard," Drew says. "Here's the thing, I happen to be Knowsley's reigning champion of thumb war. I'm undefeated, and I'm known to take on all comers."

"Like who?"

"Like my niece."

"Right then," Tom says, shaking off the doubt that had crept into his eyes. "I've no idea where Knowsley is but you're in California now, Pops, so let's get to it. One round and the winner takes all, and by that I mean the bed." Tom grasps

Drew's hand and wraps his fingers around it. Both men point a tensed thumb straight up in the air.

"International rules. No cheating," Tom says. "Ready?"

Drew nods.

"One, two, three, four – I declare a thumb war!"

Two opposing wibbling, wobbling, wrestling thumbs lean in, lean back, dive for the pin, slip out and lurch at each other. Tom's sticks out his tongue. Drew's right cheek clenches and he can't help but blink ferociously. Both warriors squeeze their grip, tendons in wrists stand proud.

"Ha! One, two and… three! That's a pin!" Tom Pushes his thumb on Drew's defeated digit.

"Well, bugger my life." Drew flaps his hand in the air.

"The winner, and still undisputed champion – *Thomas Cake*!" shouts Tom, as if he were announcing his victory to an arena crowd. He presents his thumb high in the air, first to one side of the room, then to the other, imitating the blare of 10,000 people. With victory properly celebrated, he approaches his prize. He leans down, reaches his arms underneath the bed, and tries to lift it. His face twists with struggle.

"What now, Thomas Cake?" Drew asks.

"Call me Tom. I won the bed, but I don't want it here. I'm going to…" he pauses, giving all his strength to the struggle. "I'm going to move it to the corner."

The bed doesn't move at all.

"Allow me," Drew says.

"Don't do it! Don't help me. I've got this," Tom gasps.

"You most certainly haven't, son." Drew crouches and inspects the bed's legs

"A man doesn't require help unless he asks for it. I can look after myself. If you hear me ask for help, then help. If not, never ever try. A man has to face his challenges head on."

"Why?"

"Because when I set out to do something, I mean to do it single-handedly. If you take away a man's struggle, you rob him of his victory."

Tom's face flushes beet red, his neck, cheeks and eyes are tight with the effort of lifting. "I don't need pity. I've always had to take care of things myself. I'm an orphan, you know." He strains his words, and his face gets even redder.

"Tom, going at life all alone is a terrible way about things. You'll realize that when you're older. You'll learn that struggling alone is pointless. For instance, this bed of yours – it's bolted to the ground."

"Oh." Tom releases the bed and stands up, breathing heavily. "You know what? I think that bed looks great where it is."

"No parents then? Sorry to hear that," Drew says, still looking under the bed.

Tom wipes the effort off his brow. "It's hardly your fault. You do look familiar though. What's your name again?"

"Drew Samuel."

Tom knots his face and murmurs, "Not *Drew Samuel* – the DJ?"

"You've heard of me?"

"Yeah. I remember, about ten years ago, that song was everywhere. What was it called? One second, I'm sure it's on the tip of my tongue."

"Churchill," Drew offers.

"Why did you do that? Don't tell me! Now let me think. The song was called… Churchill, yes, correct. I heard it everywhere when I was, like, nine years old. How come you didn't release anything after that?"

Drew screws up his chin. "I released seven albums after that."

"Not very good ones, I suppose?"

Drew chokes back a laugh. "Suppose not."

"How come you ended up in this bunker?"

"I basically just kind of, ended up here. What about you? Do you know what happened to your parents?"

"They're dead, I guess." He sits on the bed and drags his bag over.

"No foster parents or anything like that?" Drew sits across the room, on his losers' bed.

Tom looks into space. "Yeah, for a little while. I was always fighting with the other kids in the orphanage, so they sent me to a big family across town that used to adopt kids for kickbacks. I don't know how it worked, but the government would give them money to take in children, so they took as many as they could and made a business out of it. Food and clothes hurt the company's bottom line, I guess, so me and the other kids never had much of anything. We all used to sleep in the basement." He unzips his bag. "One day I had enough, so I ran away, naturally, but only back to the orphanage. It was the only other place that existed in my world. You should have seen the look on the faces of the staff when I turned up! They wanted to take me back to the family, but I refused – kicking and screaming like only a little boy can. After I promised to stop fighting, they said I didn't have to go back, but on one condition

- I'd have to work for my bed. So, I'd cook and clean and do anything they needed around the place. That's how it was."

"You still live there?" Drew says.

"No. A few years later, a man and woman came asking after a little girl – Cindy, they said her name was. The orphanage said they couldn't help, but it didn't stop the couple from coming around every week and asking questions.

"I knew her, she was in that family with me, in the basement, so I told them what I knew and they went looking and found her there, in the basement, half starving. They reported the foster parents and the whole thing was in the papers, 'Local foster family found guilty of neglect', or something. I don't know what happened to the other kids. The orphanage started paying me for my work after that, and they put me in a school. I'm in college now. That's why I have these."

He plunges an arm inside his bag and produces four textbooks. "These are my future, business and economics. It took all my savings, but I enrolled on a course at Cal State. I'll be getting a CBE in business and economics. And that's how I'm going to make a success of my life. The foster home I work at is part of the church, so I was told about this place and brought here. This bunker's somewhere to ride out the hurricane, probably as good as any other place."

Drew stretches and yawns. The bed is comfortable, soft. "Can I ask you a question?"

"Fire away, Pops." Tom says, leafing through on of his books.

"Do you believe the Pastor? I mean, the things he says?"

Tom laughs. "Hell no. I don't even think the Pastor believes the things he says anymore. He's insane. You heard him earlier.

He wasn't always like that. He used to preach the gospel, the Bible and that's all. But then he went away for a few years on a mission to Brazil. The rumor was he was actually in a mental asylum, but who knows? He came back and started a charitable foundation, which he used to buy the orphanage and other places. Then he started to change.

"Since he came back, he wants people to worship him more and more, and everything he does is staged to get attention. He'll go very far out of his way to help you, to make you indebted to him. I've seen it time and again since I was little, and usually that's enough to make people love him. He's got the power and money to make things happen. I suppose it's not bad, really, if good things come of it. In one way, he's like a genie, or maybe the devil – he'll make your wish come true if you give him your soul. If being nice doesn't work, he'll be aggressive to get your attention, to get your loyalty. He's clever like that. He can analyze people and see that they're weak too."

Drew feels the pull of sleep. "What are you weak to, Tom?"

"Nothing."

18

THE PAST IS GONE

"Hold, two, three. Up to the ceiling."

Blinking, bleary and altogether out of sorts, Drew rolls over in his bed and opens a fuzzy confused eye to the noise in his room. From his pillow, he sees some strange movement.

"Up to the ceiling. Down on the ground. Hold, two, three, and back up to the ceiling!" Tom's gasping for air and midway through some sort of performance.

"What are you doing?" Drew asks.

"This is what they do in the special service. It's how the green berets stay in shape. They're famous for it."

"Are they now?"

"I'm glad you're finally awake. You snore so much I was thinking about twisting your ears."

"I don't snore." Drew covers his head with his pillow.

"Yes, you do. And you fart in your sleep too. I think you farted yourself awake at one point."

"Was that what that was? I thought we had a burglar."

"A farting burglar?" Tom smirks and stops his exercise, resting his hands on his thighs. "Come on," he says, "let's get a shower and some breakfast and start the day properly."

Drew throws his pillow on the floor. "If we must."

"We have to at some point, so it might as well be now."

"Righto." Drew rolls out of bed and trips over Tom's rucksack. "What's that doing over here?"

"I threw it at you to stop you snoring. You're a very heavy sleeper."

"That's true. It's a special skill I've honed over many years of sleeping on tour buses. You roll and jostle around something awful on a tour bus bed. You feel every pothole on the road, and every gear change from the driver. Every bit of steering and rumbling can be felt through the thin mattress in a bunk the size of a coffin. Even without booze, I can sleep a hurricane away in a stationary bed like this one. This room is a real leg-up from a tour bus."

"You make touring sound terrible."

"You get swept up in it, and the trouble is before long you get dependent on it, and after ten years of touring you get stuck. What else is a thirty-two-year-old DJ supposed to do?"

"Business and economics," Tom pats the books by his pillow.

"I don't know if I'm fit for that. It might be too late for me. You study hard, Tom, make something of yourself, and don't be like me."

"I won't." Tom smiles.

"I'll probably end up a roadie," Drew says. "I don't mind that. You know, lately, I've started to feel that my touring habits are proving disadvantageous in the normal world, in the fixed urban life, I mean."

Tom looks up from his books, "You're not all that bad, you know. You can always do something else with your life. Don't let your past define you."

"You're a wise one, young Tom. Here I am, harping on about my hardships to an orphan, no offense."

"None taken. Now stop being pathetic."

"Fat chance. Ah, let's get food. I'm starving. Maybe at breakfast I'll find that woman I came here with. I saw her on the streets last night and offered her a lift. I haven't seen her since. I hope she's OK."

"She'll be fine. If she made it inside, not much can go wrong. Mother will have found her a room and she'll be bunking with someone and doing what we're all doing – waiting for the hurricane to end. Now, come on, let's get on with the morning."

19

DIARY OF COURTNEY WEAVER.
MARCH 2021

I'm not sure what date it is, but I suppose it's morning now. I'm not sure where I am, but I suppose I'm safe. Fortunately, I was able to get some paper and a pencil from the children. They are all such sweet little things, I don't think they realize there's a hurricane outside, or maybe they don't care. I don't blame them. I don't care, either. I should have stayed outside and let the hurricane take me to Ethan.

I'm in a bunker of some kind. It has a strange damp smell, but I'm getting used to it now.

I have no perception of the hurricane from inside here. The walls are very thick, made of concrete. I haven't seen a TV or a radio, and I don't remember where I put my phone, or my bag. I've lost all contact with the outside, and with who I used to be. I'm slipping away.

There's at least half a day that I can't account for. Immediately after Ethan passed, I waited and waited for help. Eventually, the police and later the ambulance came. From that point, I remember Ethan being loaded into an ambulance, and that's all.

When I arrived in this bunker the Pastor greeted me personally. His wife gave me a bed to sleep in. There's nothing extraordinary about the room. It's small and basic. The bed seems comfortable enough. The frame looks homemade, it's unpainted, rough wood. The sheets look handmade too. They're garish brownish-orange color, with a circular orange pattern that would've been normal in the 1970s. But they're comfortable and well made. Someone worked hard to make these. The sheets seem to be a conspicuous attempt to relax the space, but they do little to make up for the lack of windows. The light is dim from one bulb. A large loudspeaker is mounted on the wall between the beds. The Pastor wasn't lying when he said he had a PA system. There are speakers everywhere. I bet he can talk to every corner of every room.

Each bed sits at opposite ends of the room. There's enough space between the beds for them to feel separated, which is good because I share the room with another woman. She seems nice and quiet.

There's food at this place, but it doesn't seem like much, judging by our first meal. There's lots of other people here too, maybe hundreds. A very pregnant girl gave birth as soon as we arrived. She's the wife of the man I'm going to kill. He works here as the cook. I hope breakfast is nice.

20

DO NOT STAND IN A PLACE OF DANGER TRUSTING IN MIRACLES

This morning is a very different morning than any other Hazel can recollect. Today, there'll be no Flynn to sit on her desk like a pile of work. There'll be no office at all, for that matter, and no beach, no sunshine, no sky. She'll have only the cracked concrete ceiling above her. Its cold expanse her new horizon, its dangling bulb is her new sun.

Her normal morning commute, usually a calming walk along the beach, is a distant memory, a place she wasted with morning frustrations. Today, all she has is a brisk, shoeless walk to a damp shower block.

She taps her feet and waits in line for a shower cubicle. Listening to the sound of someone else's shower from behind a closed door, she realizes that her usual trials and tribulations are gone, and she misses them dearly. This new, temporary life inside the concrete block feels as if it belongs to somebody else, and these circumstances feel as if they're under someone else's control. If it were her choice, she wouldn't have to line up for an overused lukewarm shower, and she wouldn't have to dry her body with a towel too small for its purpose. In fact, she wouldn't have come to this place at all. She'd be in a known place with known challenges that wouldn't present such a puzzle to the nerves.

Too many questions, apprehensions, and worries swim in the current of her thoughts. As the shower pours, so to do her anxieties, first as single drops, then as a deluge, and the uneasy stream springs from many places: The Pastor's beliefs, his unknown intentions and the fervor of his followers. These things distract, occupy and swell into a new feeling she has no name for, one of fatigue and constant dreadful calculation, of weighing up likelihoods of conflict, mixed with the inclination to present a friendly exterior to the people around her that have been so kind, yet seem so dangerous in their collective intensity.

Drying herself, she grows sure that her apprehensions are valid, and one by one, they will make themselves known. Dressing in yesterday's clothes, she composes herself for her first full day as a citizen of Salvation and for the first undefined danger to reveal itself.

21

HOPE IS A GOOD BREAKFAST

"This is shit," Drew says, running his fork through his breakfast.

"It is supposed to be edible, though." Tom scoops the heavy yellowish-gray sludge off his plate with a fork. "But would it hurt to have some bacon for breakfast?" He eyes the food warily and takes a bite. "It's obviously made from a powder mix, and it's really buttery, but not that bad."

Drew sniffs his plate. "Smells odd, but I'm too hungry not to eat."

"Wash it down with coffee and you won't notice." Tom eats heartily, having discovered this method of tolerating the meal.

"Hey, Tom." Drew grins. "Look over there. Here come more people. When they go to the kitchen's serving hatch, watch their faces when they see what the food's like."

Two older men and two old women enter the room. They amble their way to the serving hatch, pick up an empty plate and hand it to Sid, who takes up a silver ladle in one of his tattooed hands and scoops a heap of slosh from a deep tray and drops it on the plate. Then, for a brief moment, a moment that could be easily missed, the diner's mouths crinkle, their chin shrinks, and their eyes widen with exaggerated displeasure.

"Aww, bless them," Tom says. "And here comes another one. Oh, wow, look at her."

"Who?" Drew follows Tom's eyes to the serving hatch. "Yeah, that's Hazel."

"You know her?"

"I met her yesterday. She's ok."

"She's more than ok, Drew." Tom's fixed his eyes on her. "She's more than ok."

"Calm down and eat your breakfast."

Hazel's wet hair is slicked back and draped over one shoulder. Drew watches Tom checks out Hazel's pencil skirt and her fitted blouse as she leans into the serving hatch for idle chitchat with Sid.

Tom flicks a thumb at Drew. "Right. Thumb war it is then."

"For what?" Drew rests his chin on his palm and rubs his silvery stubble.

"She's nice. I like her and it's *obvious* you do, so we thumb war. The loser isn't allowed to, you know, get in the way. It's the only honorable thing to do," Tom says, waving his fork.

"Obvious?" Drew says.

"Yes, obvious. Therefore, thumb war."

"I'm not sure that's how these things work, Tom." Drew moves his rubbing to the back of his neck.

"Ah, so you do like her. You didn't deny it. I rest my case, your honor." Tom takes an emphatic bite of cold sludge from his fork and shows off the silvery utensil, as if it were the concluding piece of evidence in an investigation.

"Yeah, she's good looking, but…"

"But nothing," Tom says, charging his words. "Thumb war!"

"Oh, Tom."

"Thumb war! You're scared. That's what this is."

"Righto, son. Brace yourself for a right thumb-kicking."
Drew reaches out his hand across the table, which Tom eagerly
takes.

"One, two–" Tom begins.

"No, no. It's my turn," interrupts Drew. "A-one, two, three,
four, I declare a thumb–"

"That's cheating!"

Drew attacks with a tensed thumb and goes for a surprise
pin.

"I should have seen that coming, with the stakes being as
high as they are." Tom pushes his tongue out of the side of his
mouth and clamps it with his lips. He forces Drew's attack
away with a swipe.

"It'll do you no good, Tom. And! Here. It. Is." Drew leans
forward, lifting off his chair to gain a height advantage and
presses Tom's thumb down for a certain, yet controversial,
victory.

"The winner and new undisputed world champion – Drew
Samuel!" Drew announces his victory with too much
satisfaction. He lifts his thumb into the air. "Taught you a
lesson that time, didn't I, son?"

Tom shakes the defeat out of his hand. "We'll have a
rematch. You cheated. Such a dirty player."

"Over here, Hazel. Sit with us." Drew waves her over.

She takes the free seat beside Drew. "Morning."

"Hi. My name's Tom."

"Hi, Tom. Quite a spread for breakfast, isn't it?" she says.

"It could be worse, I suppose. I'm not sure how, but it could
be," Tom says. "Did you sleep well?"

Listening to Hazel's response, a question in Drew's mind,
but before its shape emerges, the loudspeakers on the wall come

to life with a thud, a crackle, and a whine. Finally, the Pastor's amplified voice is thrown into the corner of every room.

```
"Morning, Salvation. I trust this morning
finds you in good health. I bring glad
tidings and genuine love to all within the
sound of my voice. Today is a momentous
day, it's the beginning of our new lives
and the breaking of a new dawn. The
devastation outside is total. The
destruction is unprecedented. You wouldn't
believe it. It's much worse than anyone
expected, and the hurricane is still at
its work, but here in Salvation, we can,
together, live well and live long. We will
have a special sermon tonight at seven.
Until then, please get along in a spirit
of kindness and gratitude. That is all."
```

"Right then, Pops. I'm going to hit the books," Tom says. "Hurricane or no hurricane, you got to have discipline. Hazel, it was nice to meet you." Tom takes his plate, and as Hazel looks down at her breakfast, flashes a thumb at Drew and mouths the word "rematch".

Drew shrugs it off. "I've been thinking about what you said the other night, about love, hopes and dreams. Do you remember?"

"I do." Hazel sneers at the mush on her plate.

"I was speaking to Tom last night. He's an orphan, you know?"

"Aww," she says, lowering her fork, "That poor guy…"

"Yeah, Tom's great. Point is, I don't have it that bad, really, and maybe I've become a little cynical in my old age."

"OK, old man." She prods her plate. "I can't blame you for being a bit cynical. Look at the place we're in – and we're stuck in here. Maybe being cynical is normal when things aren't great. It's like a warning sign." She pulls her phone from her skirt pocket, lays it beside her breakfast and taps the screen.

"Maybe," Drew watches her stare at her phone, "but I think being cynical becomes a habit, and that can't be good, can it?"

"Then change," Hazel says, not looking up from her phone. "How old are you? Thirties? If you don't like being cynical, there's plenty of time to change." She shakes her head, swipes her phone and tuts.

"I suppose so. All we have is time right now, while we wait for the hurricane to pass." Drew gazes into the middle distance. "We're rich in time here. We have time to waste, time to share, we can make it or spend it."

"Time makes cowards of us all," Hazel says, half listening. She purses her lips, eyes still on her phone.

"I think that was 'fatigue'," Drew says. "Time makes us bolder."

Hazel looks up. "Do you think that's true?"

"It seems unlikely to me. How can time make you bolder if it wears you away with fatigue? Time always wins. It sees everybody dead."

"Time is a weapon?" she mutters.

"Maybe it's this; time destroys everything," Drew waves his fork like a wand.

She waves a dismissive hand. "I think we'll find out what time does for ourselves over the next few days. I don't like this place at all. The people, the Pastor, this food, it all gives me the creeps."

"Yeah, that Pastor-guy, he's not right. He's definitely bilking these people out of something, I'll bet."

"Bilking?"

"Yeah, it's a word. It'll get you top points in Scrabble."

"Scrabble?"

"Yeah, the board game."

"What's a board game?"

"Forget it," Drew says, conceding everything.

"I will. I'm desperate to forget all of this and fast forward my life by two or three days. The hurricane will be over then and I can leave, and I'll never have to see any of these people ever again."

"Ah," Drew says, breaking in with rhythm, "now, that's something I know you can't do, unfortunately. It's one of the universe's built-in limitations. No fast forwarding, or rewinding, or pausing. If I could rewind time, what would I do? Actually, no, I wouldn't rewind – that would be awful, I'd have to do everything again. I'd fast forward instead, yeah, right to the end and see how it all turns out. And then I'd rewind back to here. I think I'd lead a happier life that way. There would be no mysteries about the end. I think that's where all anxiety comes from, the fear of death. If I go forward and see that I die aged a hundred on a nice bed at home surrounded by a loving family, that'll be fine for me."

"But what if you don't see that? What if you see that you'll die tonight? The victim of a bloody murder, all alone and nobody sees you. Nobody sees your pain."

"Wow." Drew slumps like a kite on a calm day. "I think I'd do things differently in the time that I've got left. I'd make the most of it."

"Oh, I know what that means. It means you'd have one last fuck, doesn't it?" Hazel says, lifting her fork to her lips.

"Yeah, it does. What's wrong with that? What else can be done with so little time in this place? Falling in love would be pointless. I don't have time to win a Nobel prize or score the winning goal in the World Cup final or figure out what the world sees in Kim Kardashian. Of all the things on the bucket list, having more sex is probably the only practical thing I have time for. I could use the time to have sex, then write my will."

"So, who are you going to sex-up?" Hazel says, brimming with the gossipy silliness of the Wolf and Cellar's Sunday afternoons.

"I'd probably ask for volunteers," considers Drew, "then, to narrow down the field from that presumably large pool of people, I'd draw a few names out of a hat to decide the lucky winners."

"Winners? Plural?"

"I'm about to have a bloody death, so I might as well. Oh, I'm going to miss everything so much. Sex, obviously, breakfast burritos, music, my couch, trees, books and the smell of old words, the sounds of clinking change in my pocket, the sun, cherry blossoms, birdsong, being alive, really. I'll miss it all."

"In that case, you better make today count. What are you going to do?"

"That's my problem. I never really have plans. But I can change that." He looks around the room. "Today, I'll mostly be… playing dominoes – with you!" Sensing a refusal, Drew continues, "Come on, I'm about to die and all you're doing is staring at your phone. It'll do you no good. We're in a bunker, the walls are so thick you'll never get a signal in here, and if you did, who are you going to call? And what can they do in a hurricane? Save your battery for when the hurricane's passed. Come and help me live life to the fullest by playing the crap out of those dominoes over there."

The day passes, first with dominoes, then with cards, then with some talk of DJ'ing and then of government science. Then food; soup, "Delicious Hat Soup", according to Drew's reading of the handwritten menu on the wall, but after tasting, Hazel determined its flavor was actually tomato. Later, when the day was assumed to move into the early evening, and after another meal of rice, peas, and carrots and another speaker announcement by the Pastor, the band arranged themselves and played as they had done the night before, with bluesy popular mellow standards from a bygone era.

"You can't die without a last dance." Hazel smiles, there's mischief in her eyes, "Let's dance."

"Let's dance? Who do you think you are, David Bowie? I can't dance. I don't know how."

Hazel's expression is defiant, and Drew quickly caves. "OK, fine, just don't make fun of me."

"Shut up and come on, I love this song," she walks him to the dance floor.

"What song is it?" Drew asks.

"'When a Man Loves a Woman', probably one of the most famous songs ever. Some DJ you are. I'm beginning to doubt your credentials."

"I'm more of a dubstep kind of guy."

"Well, Mr. Dubstep, if you're going to die tonight, one last dance is only fair. Now, hold my hands and move your feet slowly, like this. Not like that. You have no coordination at all. Come on *co-ordo-boy*, watch me and follow my lead."

Dancing, hand in hand, Drew finds his step, and after many hours of conversation, food, and laughter, the light of a bond suggests itself. For the first time in as long as he can remember, he finds himself face to face with something that absorbs him completely. No fractures in his mind appear, no obscure memories, no interruptions, just dancing with Hazel, looking into her eyes and her looking into his.

"Do you feel that?" Hazel asks.

"Yeah. I think I do."

"Creepy, isn't it?"

"Creepy? That's rude. I thought we were having a nice time."

"I don't mean that. I mean *them*. Look around!"

The crowded room, which a moment earlier was rich in dancing and joviality, is now poor in both. The packed room is flooded with stares, and all rivers flow towards Drew and Hazel.

"I don't think they like me," Hazel says, halting their dance and leading Drew to a chair.

"I don't think it's you. I think it's me," Drew whispers.

"You mean for hitting that guy with your car?"

"Maybe. Very likely. I wonder what happened to him?"

22

THERE IS NO PART OF MY LIFE, UPON WHICH I CAN LOOK BACK WITHOUT PAIN

Stephen is in Salvation's humble medical facility. It has three beds surrounded by instruments and apparatus. The temperature's cool, and there's a strong sharp smell of isopropyl alcohol. Stephen wakes. A nurse stands over him. The light's too bright.

"Don't worry," the nurse says, "Father's going to take care of you soon. In the meantime, I'll make sure you're comfortable. How's your pain?"

"It's fine, honestly," he says. "I think I got off pretty lucky... I just had my bell rung pretty hard. Where am I exactly? How long was I out for? Has the hurricane passed?"

His head hasn't felt this bad since his first hangover at age fourteen, when, egged on by his friends, he chugged half a bottle of whiskey. His brain was still swirling the next day when he got on the mound to pitch in his junior league baseball game. Smelling of last night's booze, he tried to keep it together with deep, slow breaths, but the day was baking hot, and breathing only made the sickness worse. He pulled his cap down as far as it would go and squeezed the baseball, concentrating on his grip, then he puked all over his shoes. The coach wasn't happy, and the crowd burst into laughter.

The worst of it was the headache. It felt like rhythmic lightning strikes to the head, like the brain was trying to figure it out, firing out SOS signals and swirling into oblivion.

Now, lying in this hospital bed, he has the same energy-sapping headache. He tries to open his eyes again, but the lights hanging from the ceiling still hurt. His bed is comfortable, and some kind soul has pushed a space heater bedside him, he can feel its heat.

"You've been out cold all night," the nurse says.

"Did anybody get my boots? I think lost 'em in the mud out there," he says, rubbing his forehead.

"Yes, we cleaned them up for you. They're almost as good as new, but I'm afraid you won't be wearing them anytime soon."

"What do you mean?" He opens his eyes to the blinding light, shading his eyes. He looks down to his feet and wiggles his toes but gets distracted by a plastic tube coming out of his arm. His eyes follow the tube into a plastic IV bag.

"Am I paralyzed?"

"Oh no, nothing like that. Don't worry. I can see your toes move," the nurse says.

He looks down to check for himself and he's relieved to see his toes wiggle. Images of wet mud, bare feet, car headlights, and a gurney flash through his mind. He can still see flecks of mud under his fingernails, and he realizes someone must have cleaned him up, probably this nurse. She must have also changed him into the white gown he has on.

"…Thank you for your kindness, but I'll be getting up now. I need a leak." He rubs his eyes and tries to focus on the nurse again. Below her cap is a plain but not unattractive face. She's maybe twenty-five and dressed in what looks like a nurse's uniform, but not a modern one. It's dated like a hand-me-down, or something found in an old military surplus store. It's over-washed powder blue, with darker blue buttons and matching trim around the arms. A white-faced silver clip-on watch dangles from the breast of her shirt. A name tag reads "Nurse Chamberlin".

She inspects the bag of his IV. Her demeanor is cold and clinical.

"Could you point me in the direction of the bathroom?" Getting up, he moves the bed covers, but shock and confusion plant him back down on the mattress. Looking at his legs, he sees he's immobilized. He looks to the nurse for an explanation.

"We had to put both your legs in casts – it really was necessary." She flashes a smile, and a perverse brightness rises in her face. Stephen's surprise transforms into confusion, then into terror. She continues to talk, but he isn't quite able to listen.

"It's all right, lie back. I've numbed you right out. You can't feel a thing. You're a lucky boy. You don't know how lucky you are. Father's going to come for you now."

She readies a needle and checks the chamber against the light, then stabs the tip into the thin plastic wall of his IV bag and pushes the plunger all the way down.

Moments begin to slip and stutter. The room draws distant. The air in Stephen's lungs grows thick and difficult, and his ears fill with cotton wool. His hands grope into deep space and he claws at the nurse's clothes, the coarse fabric slips between his fingers. He watches his last conscious moment from a high place as babbling sounds leave his lips; what he's trying to say, he doesn't know. His body is powerless. The lights above his bed glow dimmer and dimmer until his willingness to resist fades and his mind is overwhelmed. SOS. SOS. SOS.

"Salutations to all within Salvation. This evening's sermon will be a special one. In ten minutes, everybody must gather in the Sermon Hall to witness a miracle. Tonight, our faith and our father's power will heal the broken legs of a cripple. That is all."

23

YOU HAVE BEEN HEALED

Every face turns to a loudspeaker, every eye narrows with the weight of cognition, and without a pause, every soul makes its way to the Sermon Hall.

It doesn't take long for the room to fill and for a chattering spirit to form. The air in the Sermon Hall is cold, yet a few elderly parishioners fan themselves. There's a pamphlet waiting on every pew. Hazel picks one up and scans the glossy printed page. "The Sermon of Salvation and Damnation" reads the title. Below is a list of "Rules":

1) Do not speak ill of Father
2) There shall be no gods before Father
3) Show kindness
4) Mother is Father's wife. There will be no jealousy towards her
5) Report anyone who tries to talk to you about leaving
6) Report anybody that speaks ill of Father or of Mother or of Salvation
7) The Planning Committee rules with the will of Father

Along the bottom edge are the words: "Father carries a great burden of Salvation," and "Father is a mighty power. Thank Father we are here."

The Pastor enters the hall, and all heads turn and greet him. He smiles, shakes hands, and makes his way down the aisle. A long white scarf hangs from his shoulders. His strong frame, outlined by his black silken gown, shimmers in the light. His broad smile is reflected in all the faces around him.

In his wake, walk eight church members, tall and proud. He takes his place behind the microphone and pauses to calm the people with an expressionless gaze. He signals to little Karis Fletcher, and she joins him at the front. In her yellow dress, she stands before the crowd and sings:

> "Little baby, as you grow old,
> I want you to drink from the plenty cup,
> I want you to stand up tall and proud,
> I want you to speak up clear and loud, my little baby."

She's accompanied by the flat-sounding dusty piano, and her melody finds favor as it haunts, fades, and leaves a moment of reflection in its place.

The Pastor breaks the silence.

"Dear friends, how I love you."

A spontaneous clapping of hands.

"Today, we gather to celebrate a miracle birth – the first child born in our new paradise, in our Salvation. Baby Quincy Jr is a miracle. There can be no doubt. Quincy Jr is pure, and we welcome him to this new world as only we can."

More warm applause follows. Easter stands to show her child. The Pastor stiffens his posture and grips the lectern's edge. With glassy eyes and slicked black hair, he stares.

"There are things that this beautiful child will never know, and this blessed, precious child will be better for it. He's born into a perfect land, and he will never know that life outside this Temple is hell, and life away from Father's love is hell, and nothing can be accomplished without Father."

A cordial smattering of hands ensues. The Pastor moves on in a warmer voice.

"As I always tell you, love is a healing remedy. Now, let us fill this room with love. Let our minds be open and our hearts be full."

As the crowd stands and greets each another, a puzzled expression appears on the Pastor's face. Something appears to have disturbed him. He peers through the multitude and focuses on an elderly woman. "Sister... Sister Clare. Dear sister... I see you have four sons, and your fifth son died of cancer? Is that right?"

Clare grasps and knots the hem of her blouse. "My second son..."

"I mean, the son who is not living. He, who died of cancer. He was studying to be a teacher, wasn't he? And he was so talented, and you grieved over him. I want you to be at peace, knowing that your son is safe in your father's keeping."

"Ooo, thank you, Father. Thank you, Father," drawls Clare.

"Now you have grandchildren, and you like to hold them close?"

"Yes, Father," Clare says, releasing her clothes from her creasing grip.

The Pastor removes his white scarf and holds it out. "Take this scarf and wear it. It will prevent a heart attack that lies ahead in your future. You shall be saved."

Applause, love and more applause bounce off the walls, the ceiling, and the floor. Clare takes the scarf and returns to her seat. Her face is marked with tears.

"Ida May Kips," says the Pastor, peering about the room, "you're from Corpus Christi, Texas?"

"Yes."

"Your maiden name is 'Pleasant'? And you say in your mind that you try to live up to that name, but people make it difficult?"

"Yes."

"Father knows the pain you've suffered. My spirit was with you when you lost your three cousins, distant cousins, nearly all at the same time."

"Yes."

"And you lost your mother in 2007?"

"Yes."

"You have a pants suit. Two-piece with a gold pattern. You have it with you. You packed it for your trip to Salvation?"

"Yes."

"I'm now looking into the future to change events that would have happened to you in your life... Listen to my words – do not wear that pantsuit until after the sixteenth of April and be careful. Do not fear. If you do these things and always think about how very, very much your father loves you, all will be taken care of."

The crowd roars and the Pastor allows the noise to linger, but not for long.

"I've sincerely and conscientiously not only attempted to prove, but I have proven, that you cannot base your faith on the Bible. Do you get what I have just said here? Until something has been proven empirically, whatever your conceptual ideals, you have to make a juxtaposition with reality someplace, so you know by evidence that it's tested to be real. And today, I will give you all more evidence of my power. We have with us an unfortunate poor man who was knocked down by a car right in front of us, right outside the doors of Salvation. We owe it to this man to channel our spirit to heal his body. We owe it to that man, so bring him out here. Bring that man to me."

Nurse Chamberlin appears at the back of the room. Her shadow stretches up the aisle, and in her shade is a wheelchair. She pushes it towards the lectern. The sight of it, or rather its occupant, causes a stir. People stand and point and marvel.

Stephen sits in the wheelchair, slumped and dressed in white. His head is bowed, his arms limp, his legs covered with a white sheet and pointing straight ahead. His eyes are open but vacant and rolling. The crowd is excited.

Nurse Chamberlin pushes Stephen to the front of the room.

Hazel ducks below the attention of the crowd and whispers, "Drew! That's the guy you hit. He looks bad!"

"Look at his eyes..." Drew mutters.

"Look at his legs!" Hazel says.

The Pastor stokes the energy in the room. "This poor man sits before us, uncomfortable, in pain, unable to walk. His bones have suffered many breaks, many breaks, and fractures. His legs have been destroyed by a speeding automobile, and his body is beyond repair without the love of Father. Now, Sister! Show me his legs!"

Nurse Chamberlin whips the sheet off Stephen's legs, exposing the two crude homemade casts. People, alive and animated, expecting and bouncing, stop and suck the air with a collective breath.

"Let us, with love, heal this man! Watch Father's glory!" the Pastor yells.

The people rise and clap. The piano provides discordant energy to the atmosphere.

The Pastor walks a few circles around the wheelchair, scanning it up and down. He stops at Stephen's stiff bound legs and places one hand above the casts. He makes a tight fist and raps his knuckles on the plaster. The impact can be heard throughout the hall. He opens his hand and moves it in circles above Stephen's legs. He narrows his eyes and adds a second palm to the motion, shouting, "Be healed! Be healed! Be healed! Bumwilamub-batoo! Be healed!"

He raises his hands to the sky as if to pull out the pain and injury, and announces, "This man is healed! Cut off these casts, and this man shall walk! Now! Do it now!"

The room is wild with emphatic declarations. Alarmed by the crowd, Stephen's head bobbles and he gazes at the people with dead eyes.

For Stephen, time passes in slow bursts of unsynchronized sound and movement, as if someone is badly editing the reel of his reality.

Someone's cutting my legs! What is that on my legs? Why am I here? What's going on?

Scissors cut through the thin casts and expose his fleshy, white-power blemished legs. He's lifted to his feet. Someone takes away the chair, and a sudden surge of encouraging cheers pushes him further into uncertainty and fear.

Who's holding me? Why? Who are these people? Why are they clapping?

"Walk!" commands the Pastor.

Stephen stands and sways.

"Walk! You shall walk with the love of Father!"

He feels distorted and confused. The crowd hushes. They watch him watching them. His legs stutter and balk in spasms, trying to keep balance, he motions a step forward and the crowd explodes in selfish euphoria. He walks a few drunken missteps, looking for a chair, his legs are solid, but his mind is challenged. Colors scroll across his eyes, noise fills his ears, and only narrow images of the outer world penetrate the darkness of his senses; the dull drone of a cheer, the voice of a man shouting, the sight of his legs wobbling.

What's that sound? Who is she? Where am I? Who are they?

Eventually, he closes his eyes and feels himself being wheeled away.

The sermon ends, and people flutter to the exit while Drew looks on at the lectern. He's hoping for a punchline, but all he sees is the Pastor watching and waiting. The last of the congregation leave smiling like summer dogs as Hazel shakes her head, mutters, and gets up to leave. Drew follows her lead.

If Drew has been paying any attention, he might have noticed the Pastor say a few more words into the microphone. Words that, if heard, would have caused a dreadful, sinking, submerging feeling to well up inside him, but, in this fleeting moment between thoughts, Drew's mind is elsewhere. He doesn't see the Pastor lean over the microphone, and he doesn't hear the Pastor slowly and deliberately say, "Not so fast, Drew. You and I are going to have a little talk."

24

FEAR NOT DEATH, FOR THE HOUR OF YOUR DOOM IS SET, AND NONE MAY ESCAPE IT

Drew tries to keep up with Hazel's head-down march to the corridor, but he's blocked at the doorway by two men. He follows their grim stare over his shoulder towards the Pastor, who's now flanked at the lectern by two other men with stone faces.

The pair at the door allow Nurse Chamberlin to enter, and she parades across the floor carrying glasses of wine on a tray. With a glance at Drew, she sets the tray at the lectern and whispers into the Pastor's ear. The Pastor responds in full voice into the microphone.

"OK, but if we're going to do this properly, you need to bring Oscar, Tom, and Judy back here. And, Drew, take a seat."

Nurse Chamberlin leaves.

Drew sighs. He walks back into the Hall and takes a seat directly in front of the Pastor. No words are spoken, but beat after beat, Drew looks into the Pastor's shark black eyes.

"Is this about hitting that guy with my car? I've been feeling terrible about that, but he seems ok now, I suppose."

Not a flicker of recognition passes the Pastor's face.

"Drew, while we wait, would you take some wine?"

"In a word," Drew says, "Why not."

The Pastor contracts his lips in a clear effort to resist showing some malign disapproval as he holds out a gleaming cut crystal glass that shimmers along its deep ridges. It's filled to the brim and looks like a red tulip on an elegant white stem. Drew takes the glass and for the first time notices how tall the Pastor is, perhaps six foot three.

"Quite some operation you have here," Drew says, looking around.

"Yes. I'm very proud of my accomplishments." The Pastor flourishes a gesture and looks at Drew with pensive interrogation, as if he were observing a new species. "Drew, do you understand what this place is?"

"I understand what it *was,* once upon a time," Drew says, lighting surprise on the Pastor's face.

"Oh, go on. Tell me."

Nurse Chamberlin returns with Oscar, Tom and Judy. Each is given a glass of wine. Drew takes a sip and scans the room.

"In the eighteenth century," he begins, "new punishments for crimes were being introduced in the British courts and England began sentencing convicts to transportation, which basically meant shipping criminals away to far-off parts of the world to export the problem. Out of sight out of mind, you know?"

"Yes." The Pastor signals something to the men by his side. "Continue."

"Well, before this big concrete bunker was built, this whole site was a destination for some of those British prisoners. Some of the worst offenders in the Empire were imported here to a penal colony. Back then, the empire was big, and it goes without saying there were a lot of troublemakers and generally difficult bastards. At one time, this place was a labor camp that held nine thousand people."

"Every man should have a knowledge of history. Knowledge is power, after all." The Pastor reclines on a chair brought to him by two men. "You seem to know this place in some detail. Impressive, for a drunk." His words boom through the room.

Drew takes another sip. "You see, some of my ancestors were brought here, according to the internet."

"Makes sense."

"Practically half my family tree, back in 1852. I've been fascinated with this place since I found out. In a weird way, it feels like a spiritual home. I know that's strange. Anyway, this site was part of a network of international prisons across the world, but this was the most infamous of them all. It was supposed to be escape-proof – one way in and no way out. It became notorious for two types of criminals – repeat offenders, and those who committed some of the most heinous crimes, Jack the Ripper-types, etcetera. You wouldn't believe what my ancestors did to get sent here."

"Do you think they'd be proud of the man you've become?"

"Once this place got a hold of them, who knows. You see, this place was set up to *change* people, to reform them, supposedly through work. The idea was that if a man was productive and he felt useful, he would release his criminal ways. A noble idea, I suppose, but I don't think it quite worked."

"And why's that?"

"I think it's because this place became no more than a production site – an industrial prison where convicts were forced into labor. They had to cut timber, build ships, ground grain, and the conditions were not good."

"No?"

"The inmates were assigned to different jobs. All harsh work. The worst jobs were in the flour mill. It was a big treadmill walk, you know, like, fifty or sixty men all on top of a big wheel for hours and hours every day, turning it as they walked. It was physical and psychological punishment."

"Inspired by Jeremy Bentham," the Pastor says.

"What?"

"Beating a prisoner only entrenches criminal behavior, so the world needed to find another way to repurpose their minds - work."

"You say that, but at least a beating is an upfront, obvious act with an obvious end. Jeremy's idea of redemption through work might sound nice, but it was as extreme as the old medieval punishments. He just took it in another direction and to a different end. And it didn't work."

"Of course, it didn't," the Pastor says.

"Excuse me?"

"Physical punishment is useful in reforming character, but it can only achieve so much. Using work as an alternative is really neither here nor there. The work ultimately becomes a practical necessity. No, each person is a lock that must be picked. Everyone has their own pressure point that'll reveal itself in due time. If you can pick the lock, you can make any man malleable."

"I guess."

"Of course you guess." The Pastor grins.

"So, the authorities had to build a separate prison for the men who were too rough for the rest of the inmates, a place to house the most violent and unpredictable criminals, the worst of the worst. This newer prison had thick-walled cells, a foot thick, I think, and if I'm not wrong, this bunker, in a previous life, was that prison."

"It was."

"So, where's the Hole?"

"The Hole?"

"Prisoners who misbehaved would be sent into the Hole, which is as it sounds - a hole in the ground. They'd throw prisoners in, cover it over and leave them in the dark for as long as it took for their spirit to break. Primitive solitary confinement, I suppose. Some men broke quickly. Some lasted weeks. Some told tales of a blue-eyed monster that would lurk in the dark and terrorize them."

"Do you believe everything you read on the internet?"

"Yeah. And if I'm not mistaken, right here in this room was a church hall. It was an interesting kind of church. All the pews had restraints attached to hold down the inmates, and blinders so the convicts couldn't see anyone but the priest. Very odd. Again, it didn't really work."

"But it helped many."

"It helped many to the grave. The men were pushed too far, and violence broke out. Some survived, but for those who weren't so lucky there's a cemetery known as the Isle of the Dead, where over a thousand inmates are known to be buried in a mass grave. Then, in 1867, or thereabouts, the world's most infamous prison was closed and written out of history, almost completely. Some say the bunker was maintained throughout the years by various administrations, for various reasons."

The Pastor applauds, his hand claps echo. "Well done. You're very familiar with this place, after all. That's good, a surprise, but very good." He slicks back his hair and smiles. "Drew, with your intimate knowledge of this place and your family ties to it, it's fitting, and perhaps even a little ironic, that this is where you're going to die."

The words derail Drew's train of thought. He replays the words back, scanning for sarcasm. Scanning and searching. He can't find any.

The Pastor stares at him.

"Drew, the wine you drank was poisoned. You, Tom, Judy and Oscar, you've all been poisoned. You have approximately five minutes to live, but don't worry, you'll be comfortable. It will be painless."

Drew looks across the room. Everybody's glasses are half full, or half empty, in this case. His body rises with a deep intake of breath, his chest sinks as he exhales, and inexplicably, he realizes that every inch of his body is trying to restrain laughter.

25

SHORT IS THE LIFE OF THE PROUD

Oscar, the young man and one-time usher, observes the rim of his poisoned chalice. It's wet from his lips. A single red drop stains the outside and falls to the ground a glittering red tear. His shoulders droop, his eyes lift to the heavens, then settle back to the floor. A tear drops from the corner of his eyes, followed by many more. Heartbreak, in the sound of a sigh, escapes on his breath.

"Father," he says.

"Yes, son."

"Thank you, Father. Thank you for looking out for me and giving me a second chance at life. Thank you for looking out for my momma. If it's OK with you, can I say a few words to her?"

Oscar looks at his shoes and waits for the Pastor's approval.

A blur in his periphery takes his attention. Young Tom is sprinting towards the lectern, towards the Pastor. His eyes are wide, his fists are balled, and his feet are fast across the floor.

"You evil bastard!" Tom yells.

A guard from the Pastor's side intercepts Tom and slams him to the floor. Another man grips him around the neck. Tom's face is twisted and red as he claws at the arms around his throat.

Oscar watches Tom's terrible end unfold and prays.

Not like this. Have mercy, good God, please not like this.

Constricted breathing and forced grunting fill the otherwise silent hall. More thrashing, more savage movement, more heavy breathing teaches the two men that Tom will not back down – he fights to his knees and rises against the weight of both men. The man around his neck stumbles, staggers and falls over his heels. The man around his waist falters and grabs Tom by the shirt collar. Tom resists the pull and strikes the man. With his collar torn, he stands tall and sets his eyes on the Pastor.

A guard lunges at Tom's legs and tackles him to the ground. The other, still holding a handful of his shirt, kneels on Tom's back.

"How dare you!" the Pastor shouts. "How dare you try to attack Father! Shame on you! After all I have done for you! My gosh, you never really know a person. *Oh, my gosh!*"

Tom stirs again, pushing against the knee on his spine. The Pastor speaks over the three men like an indignant father.

"Don't do this! Don't do this! Tom! Why can't you be like Judy and go peacefully into the night? Go with dignity. I command you! Have some dignity!"

Flat on his stomach, Tom tries to resist the weight on top of him, but his energy starts to evaporate.

"Have some respect, Tom. Look at Oscar and be like him," the Pastor says.

"Father, could I please see my momma?"

"Oscar," the Pastor says sharply, "rather than talk to your mother, I think it would be more appropriate if you wrote a few words down for her. I will see that she gets your letter. Let us spare her the anguish of seeing you like this."

Tears flow. Nurse Chamberlin hands him a scrap of paper and a pencil, and on his site of death he records of his final words: "Momma, I'm so sorry that this is all I leave behind. Please remember me and know that I love you. In a moment, I'm going to join Dad."

Tom's heavy breathing and the scratch of Oscar's pencil are the only mark of time moving.

"What you lack in time, you have in certainty," the Pastor says. "Bless you, my children. You are free from worry, and you are liberated from all of life's troubles. Be grateful. Let us bow our heads."

Drew looks along the pews, to the last seat on his right, to Judy. She's a plump, dark-haired twenty-something. She holds her arms in her lap, hiding her hands in the sleeves of a gray sweater that's too big for her size. Panic flashes in her eyes like a summer storm.

"You're brave," Drew says, a little too loud for the room.

She coughs, holds her head, and shrinks into tragedy.

Time is all gone, Drew realizes, no more to spend, no more to waste, none to find and it's too late to make. This is how it ends, forever. I wish I had been better.

"Congratulations, Drew, Judy, and Oscar," the Pastor says. "You all came through that test just fine."

Judy bursts into sobs. Tom tries to wriggle free again. The twisted tableau of his body eventually relaxes, and he gives up entirely.

"I had to test your loyalty, Tom. You failed. There was nothing poisonous in that wine, but you will be paying a visit to the medical bay, and you'll not be well for some time."

The two men haul Tom off, dragging him by his arms, his feet sliding behind him. The Pastor rises from his chair. "Drew, the only way to really know a man is to see him under extreme pressure, to see how he reacts under the influence of fear. You are either extremely brave or a complete fool. At this time, I'm not sure which is true."

"You know what they say,' Drew says, "you can't fool a fool, so cheers," He swigs the last of his wine and walks around the pews to collect what Judy, Oscar, and Tom had left. The Pastor watches Drew drink.

"I can see inside a man's soul. I can see every fault and every virtue, and when I look into yours, all I see is a mess. You know the saying, 'If a man is not the master of himself, then he's a servant to anybody'? Well, if ever a man needed salvation, it's you, Drew. Just what has life done to you?"

———

26

WINE IS THE ANSWER. WHAT WAS YOUR QUESTION?

Fuzzy from the wine, Drew wanders into the Common Room, looking for a chair. He sees Hazel waving him over. She's kept a seat free.

"Where the hell did you go?" she asks.

"Me? Where the hell did *you* go? I've been stuck in the Sermon Hall with that maniac. He's definitely mad. Have you seen Tom?"

"No. What's happened?"

"The Pastor pretended to poison me, Tom, and a couple of others." He glances across the room. "Tom didn't like what was going on. There was a scuffle."

"I don't like what's going on either! And a pretend poisoning? Like the pretend healing? This isn't normal. I don't know what the Pastor's intentions are, but he's dangerous, and we're stuck in here with him. What are we going to do?"

"I don't know, but I know someone who can probably give us some more information." Drew stands and waves his arms across the room. "Judy! Judy! Come sit with us."

Blurry black smudges run down Judy's cheeks. Drew's noise and animation turned all heads in her direction. To get the horrible, overexposed moment over, she walks briskly through the crowd towards Drew and Hazel's table.

"Hazel, this is Judy. Judy, this is Hazel."

"Thank you for what you said earlier," Judy says. "You dealt with being poisoned very well. Imagine if he had *actually* poisoned our drinks?" She rubs the makeup smears from her cheeks.

"This crazy pastor of yours," Drew says, "what's he about?"

Tears swim in her eyes.

"Are you OK?" Hazel says.

"No, he's, he's…" Judy looks around the room and whispers, "I can't talk here."

"I don't have the blood pressure for this," Drew says. "Don't leave us in suspense. If there's something we should know, just tell us."

"You need to leave this place if you can," Judy says, with a deliberate expression of severity, as if to transmit, without words, all her visions and memories of the Pastor.

"He's a vampire, isn't he?" Drew says.

Hazel punches his arm. "What's wrong with you?"

"Nothing's wrong with me, but I'm not so sure about Tom or Stephen. Did you see the guy Stephen earlier? Something's definitely wrong with him."

"He looked drugged out of his mind," Hazel says.

"It looked like clozapine or something like that," Judy says. "I've seen that look before. My uncle was committed to St Marc's for the good of his mental health and the safety of others after he said he heard voices in his head and attacked his neighbor with a weed whacker."

Drew sniggers. Judy continues, still wiping stray tears from her cheek with the cuff of her sweater.

"One time at St Marc's, he got mad over dinner. He threw a chair at a picture on the wall and punched the serving lady twice in the back of the head, and then he tried to spit on her. He only wanted more mashed potatoes – they were his favorite. Security tasered him then put him in lockdown. Next day, after looking him over, they said he had Intermittent Explosive Disorder, so they sedated him. After that, every time I went to see him, he had that look in his eyes." Judy turns her face and makes an earnest attempt to wipe away the last of the makeup.

"You missed a bit." Drew points at her face.

"I feel sorry for that young man," she says.

"Tom? Oh, he'll be OK. He's a fighter," Drew says.

"I've no doubt about that, but the Pastor, you don't know what he can do to people."

Drew and Hazel ask more questions, trying to elicit more details, but Judy dismisses their questions as fearful things, and as the night gathers on and with more questions going unanswered, Drew's concern for Tom grows. He scans the room again, hoping to catch sight of him.

"Tom will be OK, won't he?" Drew asks Hazel.

Her response is non-verbal, just a bare expression of slow contemplation, and it stirs him. With sullen resolve, he stands. "Goodnight, ladies. I can't stay here. I have to find young Tom."

27

BEHOLD, I STAND AT THE DOOR AND KNOCK

There's no sight of Tom in the Common Room or the Sermon Hall or the areas adjoining, so Drew searches the corridors. Each is a windowless dark tunnel flanked by closed doors. He passes room after room until he reaches the end of the dank walkway and discovers his objective; a door with a hand-painted sign reading, "Medical Facility".

He pushes the door. It's locked.

"Hello." He taps on the unvarnished wood.

"Anybody in?" He bangs on the door.

No response.

"I'm having a heart attack. Help me!"

Still no answer. He turns away from the door, but he can't let it go. He turns back and tries again. Nothing.

Having banged, kicked, and yelled, he goes to the only other place Tom might be – their shared sleeping quarters.

Tom's bed is just as he had left it, disheveled and strewn with books. Drew perches on the edge of the bed and checks his wristwatch. It's still broken.

"Could be nine o'clock. Close to ten, maybe?" he says to the empty room. "I was waiting for you to ask for help back there, Tom. I would've helped, you know that don't you? I know how you feel about that kind of thing, but I wish you'd have asked."

He glances at Tom's textbooks. "Don't feel bad about the fight. The Pastor will get over it. It's no big deal. So, he's a little insane. In fact, he's probably doing something mental right now to somebody else, and I bet he's forgotten all about that fight, or test, or whatever it was. What kind of bullshit was that anyway? So, chin up, young Tom, you're a good kid and you've got a lot going for you, but it's getting late, and the lights are due out soon, so I'll catch up with you in the morning, OK, champ?"

Drew walks to his own bed and lies on the mattress, wishing Tom would walk in the room.

"Righto, Tom, I don't know what to do, so I'm going to sleep. Don't be afraid to wake me if you come in late. Although, as you know, I'm a heavy sleeper."

He tucks himself in and takes one final look at Tom's bed as the lights snap off. In the unpurged night, thoughts creep up on him in the darkness: Tom, the Pastor, Hazel. And in the night-time black, he remembers these rooms were not built as bedrooms, but as prison cells.

Out of a hot blanket of sleep comes a shock of cold water. Drew's drenched. Water blocks his nose and forces his eyes closed. He gasps for air and wonders where the hell he is. Rubbing his eyes, he staggers to his feet and walks around the room, feeling his way along the walls, the sound of an alarm ringing in his head, morphing into a high oscillating whine. He staggers back to his bed and seeks shelter under its covers.

"Wakey-wakey, sleepyhead!" Huxley stands over him with an empty bucket and a grin.

"It's 7:20, Drew. Breakfast time. Common Room. You're late."

Drew's soaked and speechless. He's never been waterboarded before, but if it's anything like this, he's sure he'd tell you everything at the first sight of a bucket.

Huxley leaves, smiling. Tom's bed is as it was the night before: empty and littered with books.

_____

28

FEAR AND COURAGE ARE BROTHERS

Drew's ears ring long into breakfast. The noise is a high-pitched whine, exactly the sound you'd get if you struck a six-foot tuning fork against a church bell, and the result is a seemingly endless noise.

"Drew!" Hazel breaks him out of a trance. "You haven't listened to a word I've said, have you?"

"Sorry," Drew says. "But being waterboarded at 7 am is a weird way to start the day. Have you seen Tom this morning? He didn't come home last night–"

"For fuck's sake, Drew!" Hazel bangs her fork on the table.

"What?" Drew looks down at his plate.

"I said, I'm going to talk to the…" She lowers her voice and glances around. "I'm going to talk to the Pastor, and I think you should join me."

"You want to leave…?" A small voice three seats away interjects. Hazel recognizes the little girl and her yellow dress.

"Yes, we do," Hazel says. "I enjoyed your singing last night – Karis, is it? But excuse me, we're having a private conversation, so…"

Karis toys with her breakfast, "But if you leave, you won't see me sing later. I'm singing for Father again." She lifts her fork to her mouth and takes a slow bite.

Drew smiles. "Aren't you as cute as a button? Maybe we'll stick around for that."

"Plus… Father won't want you to leave," Karis says.

"I'm sure he won't, honey," Hazel says.

Karis sighs. "If you try to leave, the Blue-eyed Monster might get you."

Drew nearly chokes up his food. "You've seen the Blue-eyed Monster?" he says.

"Mom says it comes out in the dark. She says it's scary. She says my Uncle Joe saw it once, and it nearly killed him. She told me you need to be good it might get you. When it bites, it hurts you so bad it can kill." She chomps at her breakfast.

"That's an old legend, a tall tale about a monster that's supposed to haunt this place," Drew says. He looks around the room again. "Still no Tom, but here comes that moody woman from the other night."

"Who?" asks Hazel.

Tall, gaunt, and still dressed in black, the woman Drew met in the waterlogged streets floats across the room and takes a seat beside him.

"Hi, my name's Hazel–"

"Don't bother," Drew says. "She doesn't say a word. Believe me – I've tried. I'd give more than a penny for her thoughts, but it's no good trying."

She reaches for the ketchup and stares at its F-Mart's own brand tag.

"She might want to come with us," Drew says. "Let's have that chat with the Pastor. And we'll find Tom. Then you can make a call to your science buddies, and they can come and pick us up, probably in some sort of special helicopter or something. I'm sure your government people will figure it out."

Hazel lifts her fork, then lowers it back to her plate. "And if they don't? What if they can't get here, or..." She leans in. "What if we're trapped here? What if the Pastor won't let us go, and we're locked up in here like prisoners? Remember what Judy said to us last night? She said we need to get out of here, and she gave me that weird look. I wish I could find her and find out what she knows. This place isn't right. And what if the hurricane lasts for three weeks and we are trapped here? I hate doubting my own research, but–"

"Does this food taste weird to you?" Drew says.

Hazel sniffs her breakfast. "It's mush made from powder. I'm not sure how it's supposed to smell. And forget the food, I'm talking about our situation. Ah! I need to calm down and trust my data. Just three days and this hurricane will be over. That's what the data said. I can lay low for that, if it comes to it."

Drew watches the furrows on Hazel's brow grow. "Look, don't worry, we'll be fine. I've fucked up bigger gigs than this."

She finally manages to take a bite of food.

"Plus," he continues, "if there's any funny business, we can just walk out the front door. The bus driver must have a key to the entrance. It's the only door in or out that I've seen, and the driver opened it when we arrived, remember? At the very worst, we'll just steal the key from him and bail out of here."

"And where are you going to find the driver?" Hazel asks.

Drew gestures with his fork. "He's in the kitchen making the breakfast. He's the one with all the tattoos."

Hazel gazes at the kitchen and watches Sid stir a large pot.

Megan comes striding into view with a plate full of food.

"Shit." Drew lowers his head.

"Good morning, Drew, Hazel. Don't you two make a cute couple?" she says with a beaming smile. "Aww, I heard sleepyhead here had a hard time getting out of bed this morning. I hope you're finally awake."

The loudspeaker comes to life with fuzzy amplified breathing:

"Good morning and salutations to everybody... I know you are not accustomed to hearing me like this... I, I have been up all night. Someone, someone, someone tried to poison my food. Do not worry. If you're guilty, we will find you. I want everybody to be extra vigilant to people and their nef... narfa... naff... nasty intentions. Be vigilant. Spies are among us. Report all negative conversations. In better news, the laundry room is in full operation. In your room, you will find a change of clothes. Please report to your room and get changed into these new clothes. Drop off your dirty laundry at the laundry room and wear the new clothes. Today's sermon will be early, at 9 am. Don't worry, I'm in Nurse Chamberlin's care, and I am rapidly recovering. Be vigilant. That is all..."

"Screw that," Hazel says, "I'm not doing laundry here or changing clothes. I can sweat it out until I leave in a few days."

"Oh shit!" Megan feints a misstep and empties the runny magnolia mush from her plate down Hazel's blouse.

Hazel raises both arms in shock.

"I'm so sorry!" Megan says, "Now it looks like you'll have to do laundry after all." She turns and walks away.

Hazel's eyes boil.

"Yeah, she's the town bitch." Drew nods. "That is a shame, though. I liked that blouse. It was kind of see-through."

She picks up a handful of food from her chest and shows Drew a smile.

"Don't!" Drew recoils. "Calm down and eat your gruel…"

"It's not gruel! It's eggs!" She whips the mush across the table, hitting him in the face. He wipes the splatter from his cheeks and smiles, "I guess the yokes on me…"

Hazel rolls her eyes. "You're an asshole, and she's a *total* dick."

"I'll do it."

"Who said that?" Drew looks around. "She's alive!" he says, realizing the words have come from his erstwhile road companion.

"My name is Courtney Weaver," she says, still clutching the F-Mart ketchup bottle, "I'll get the keys to the front entrance, and take care of the cook in the kitchen." She puts the bottle down, and the conversation ends.

Hazel leaves to change her clothes, and as the morning matures, the quiet clinking of cutlery takes over.

29

ENTER THE VILLAGE; OBEY THE VILLAGE

Drew returns to his bedroom, wiping the last of Hazel's breakfast from his chin. There's a neatly folded garment on his bed. It's red and nylon. He unfurls it and holds it to the light.

"It's a bright red muumuu."

He takes off his shirt and his sneakers. Tom's bed has been neatly made, but his books and bag are gone, and no red gown is waiting for him. With a pang of guilt, Drew realized that in the space of hours, he's completely lost track of Tom.

He's probably changed rooms, he reasons, or maybe he's being looked after in the medical bay. Drew shudders, thinking about what could happen in this place the Pastor takes a dislike to someone.

"Tom, I want to know that you're OK, OK? Maybe just for selfish reasons, I don't know. I'm the first to admit that I don't handle guilt well."

The loudspeakers speak again:

```
"The morning sermon will be in thirty
minutes. All must be in attendance. I
repeat - all must be in attendance.
That is all."
```

～

Drew joins Hazel outside the Sermon Hall. There's a line of people walking lockstep, like segments of a centipede, and everyone is throat-to-foot in the same red gown. Some wear it well, while others look like lobsters. Drew eyes Hazel curiously.

"Why does your muumuu look better than mine? Mine looks like a bright red potatoes sack, but yours is…" His thoughts run out.

"You know where we are, right?" she whispers.

"Some concrete box in the middle of the ocean?" He looks her up and down. Her gown is tight around her waist and full around her breasts. "Wait a second– you've had your muumuu taken in, haven't you!"

"So what if I have? There's nothing wrong with wanting to look good. You could take a bit more pride in your appearance. Darlene from the sewing club took it in for me. And stop looking at my tits!" She slaps his chest. "And I asked you a question! Do you know where we are? Can't you see? We are in a C-U L T…"

"A what?"

"Take this seriously. Look around! This place… It's not right, and if we don't get out of here soon, I don't know what we're going to do. I'm scared."

Unsure of what to say, Drew gives her a hopeful smile as they walk into the Sermon Hall. The hall seems smaller than yesterday, and cracks, unnoticed the day before, run deep in the walls. The light is dimmer, and the temperature is colder.

"We're sitting at the back." Hazel pulls him into a pew.

Drew cranes his neck above the crowd, scanning it for Tom. "Ah! It's impossible! Everybody's red!" he says.

An elderly lady sits at the piano, and little Karis stands ready. The Pastor gives the signal from the lectern, and the little girls sings as the piano plays.

Drew continues to search the crowd throughout her performance, and even as the pastor begins his sermon

"Yesterday, I showed you miracles," the Pastor says, "and there will be many more great, great miracles. But today I have to address some unpleasantness. We all must realize that in this time of much trouble, the only safe place is with Father, so we've got to put an end to any rebellious or nervous talk, or we won't be able to rebuild civilization. You see, lately–"

One man, carried by his enthusiasm, stands up and cuts across the Pastor's words. "Yes, Father, 'coz I think–"

"I don't give a goddamn what you think!" Tension laces the Pastor's voice. "If we all interrupted and sounded off like you, where would we be? Now stop and keep your seat!"

The loose-lipped man sits down. The Pastor gathers venom with reflection.

"You're all outrageous. Here I am busting my ass. You all better be humble. And don't think I didn't hear you all complainin' about the food yesterday and this morning – well, I'll give you meat, don't you goddamn worry, and I don't want to hear anymore complaining or interjections."

His mood cools, and he speaks softly, almost apologetically.

"I am very emotionally disturbed. I got a lot on my mind. I stand before you with a lot on my mind – day and night, you know I get no sleep, not even for a second. None of you know about the outside forces that are working against us – the dark forces that I keep at bay. There are threats of trouble from the outside that you don't even hear about because I take care of them, but if I was to ever lose focus for one hour, just one hour, we'd all be history. That's how serious this is. I have to take special injections of vitamins in high doses to maintain my strength so I can fight for our people, such is the constant threat. It's a heavy weight of pressure on my shoulders. How quickly you would melt if you were put under the same pressure. Even in this place, I have to be careful about my food, and I look inside your souls and I can see some of you just ain't right, and it causes me worry."

He leans heavily on the lectern and takes a breath.

"Have I not always said that if you keep the right attitude, pick the right spirit and the right vibrations, you won't have to worry, 'coz I'll stir the pot, and there'll be food for everybody, there'll be work for everybody and there'll be a purpose. But we have a dark element in our midst. Not everyone is loyal. I hear talk of betraying Father and of attempts to leave this sacred place…"

The crowd boos and hisses.

Hazel grabs Drew's arm. "He means us!"

Drew's still looking for Tom.

"And for those dumb-ass fools who are not paying attention - there's a hurricane outside destroying the country! And you can't feel a thing because of my walls, my door, and my lock, but that hurricane is out there, and it's going to be out there until I'm happy that the false Gods of this world are no more!

"That's why I have the Planning Committee beside me. You will recognize them from their blue gowns. The Blue Gowns have been entrusted by me to make sure we are all on the same page. You hear a bad thing, you write it up, make a report and let them know, understand?"

The crowd nods.

A group of people joins the Pastor's side, each dressed in a brilliant blue glossy gown. The Pastor glares at the people.

"One thing you have all done is underestimate me. I made plans for treachery long ago 'coz I knew I couldn't trust nothing, and I knew that you can't put all your eggs in the one basket – so, honey, I put my eggs in many places. You figure that out if you want to. Some of you have no idea what Father is talking about. You can't even follow him, you can't even smell where he's at yet, much less follow him. You really haven't got next to it, but I've got all kinds of things in store. I've got some big plans. And you stupid piss-ants and reptiles and lower than primates can scheme all you want, but if you think you can just walk out the front door, you've got a lot to learn, sister!" His whole body tenses as he flashes sharp teeth and fleshy gums. The crowd stirs in excitement.

The Pastor lets the moment pass and resumes in a softer tone.

"Why would a person even want to go outside and return to the old life? To that society which rendered all human effort and human pain cheap and meaningless? I wonder if maybe I've been too nice? Maybe I've been too lean on some of you. See, I look at my faults analytically. I look at my past, and I see that if I'd have hated just little more, I would have had a little less trouble with you people. Sure, you got love, what are those words? – 'Hate is my enemy and I gotta fight it day and night.' What's the other line? 'Love is the only weapon?' –Shit! Bullshit! Martin Luther King died with love! Kennedy died talking about something he couldn't even understand! He was shot down! Bullshit! Love is the only weapon with which I got to fight? I got a lot of weapons to fight! And I will fight! I will fight!"

147

He passes into delirium and his eyes bulge with the pressure of new madness. The crowd doesn't applaud. Instead, they make a strange new noise, a kind of constant open-mouthed wailing, a hollow oscillation in the throat made discordant by a flickering tongue. It could be the sound of adrenaline being released into warm blood.

Drew watches the people as they hang on the Pastor's words and make his pleasure their own.

People love a showman.

The Pastor resumes. "You who don't clap. I'm watching you. I got eagle eyes. I'm watching you. Listen, brother, I'm asking you in the back, why aren't you clapping? I'm talking to you."

Drew feels ninety-nine percent sure the finger is being pointed at him.

"Now you stand by me! People wanted to nail yo' ass to the cross for something you'd done, and I covered and cared for you and I overcame the problem, and y*ou* have Gods before me? You should be ashamed of yourself."

The Pastor's eyes are wide open.

"Yooooooooou… You're out there. You can hear me. For those wanting to leave, I have one message for you – Maybe your ass should pay a visit from the Blue-eyed Monster!" The Pastor's screaming distorts the loudspeakers.

The voice of the crowd flattens to a low muttering "*Ooooh.*"

"That's right. That's all I need to say about that." He sweeps away the mood with a gesture.

Drew leans to Hazel, "Some show," he says.

"He won't let us go," Hazel says. "Did you hear him? We have to get out of here. He won't let us leave. We need to get the keys and get out of here!"

Drew places a hand on Hazel's arm and notices her goosebumps. "Look, if worse comes to worst," he says, "we'll just lay low until the hurricane passes. In the meantime, I'll speak to Courtney about getting the keys from the cook, so when the hurricane's over, we'll just walk out of here. It's going to be fine, OK?"

The cheering abates, the crowd leaves and Elvis has left the building. Hazel, still sitting in the Sermon Hall beside Drew, looks into the distance as if viewing something unfathomable. Drew rubs his forehead. They exchange deep sighs.

Karis leaves the Sermon Hall singing. The walls hold her cold refrain and add a reverberating flourish as her song rises and falls like waves.

"I feel like we've stowed away on Noah's Ark," Drew says, "and if we piss Noah off, he's going to feed us to the tigers."

"Don't make jokes. I don't understand why you aren't more concerned. This whole situation seems to wash over you." She looks at Drew like he's an irksome child.

He sighs. "I've had such a shit time recently. Nothing seems to matter anymore. A week ago, I was in Berlin, and I was convinced I'd gone mad. Long story, but one thing led to another and ended up losing my passport. I was eventually taken to the British Embassy by some hospital staff, and I had to lobby and plead all night for an emergency passport. They finally gave me one, on account of me needing it to get to the show the next day - the next show was in Budapest. This passport was six pages long, and it had a special gold cover. It was beautiful, and I knew it would fit perfectly in my collection of tour treasures.

"When I'm old and gray, I'll look through all my personal memorabilia and remember the good old times. I keep everything in a box, every AAA pass and every tour itinerary, and any other objects I find interesting. I keep all those memories stowed away under my bed as a kind of personal time capsule, only to be opened when I'm old and happy, but I'm not sure I'll make it that far. Time has a habit of making a fool out of me. So, anyway, that's where the gold passport is, in a box of memories, but it's not a happy memory. I remember sitting alone in the embassy, leafing through its pages, when as natural as a stroke, I started to cry. What's the fucking point? I thought."

The surging, swooping din inside Drew's ears returns.

30

FOOD, GLORIOUS FOOD

Drew's walked a groove in Salvation's floor, asking anyone he could find about Tom. People in the Common room claimed they didn't know anyone named Tom, which pissed him off no end, and it was a similar story in the sewing club. The storeroom staff just shrugged; the medical bay wouldn't let him in; the musicians were friendly enough and offered apologies, while others looked at him like he was crazy. By the time he found Judy, he was ready for an argument.

"Judy!"

Her face grows tight at the sight of Drew. She's all tense around the eyes, and the fingernails of her hands touch and twist as if they're trying to pull apart an invisible thread.

"Are you OK?" he asks. Noticing Judy's reluctance, he doesn't wait for an answer. "Maybe you could help me. I'm looking for a young man named Thomas Cake... Tom. He was with us last night, in the Sermon Hall, when we had that drink with the Pastor."

"You need to stop looking for him. People are talking." Her voice trembles.

"About what?"

She sets down her invisible thread and puts her hands to her throat as if to hide her words. "People are saying you're a troublemaker. It doesn't do to cause trouble. I can't say any more."

She tries to step away.

"What has the Pastor done to Tom?" he says.

"You shouldn't have come here."

"I didn't have much choice. Why did *you* come here? You don't seem to be so happy with these people."

"I have to be here," she mumbles, "before the hurricane, I tried to leave, but they forced me to come back. The Pastor's not how he appears on TV, especially when people want to leave the Temple. He had people call my home and threaten my family. I'm sorry, I don't want any more trouble. I can't say any more." She steps into the Common Room and perches among a group of ladies.

After one more check of the sleeping quarters, Drew returns to the Common Room to sit with Hazel, but he can't stop thinking about what Judy said and what she wouldn't say.

The speaker on the wall whines. The stilted voice of the Pastor follows. His speech is oddly muted, lacking the dynamism of his earlier performance:

```
"Hello, everybody. This is a reminder
- do not forget to report any strange
or   suspicious   behavior.   In   other
business,  we  have  assigned  work  duties
to  you  all.  Through  work,  we  will  make
Salvation  a  mighty  empire.  You  must
report  to  the  desk  in  the  Common  Room
after  lunch  to  be  assigned  your  role.
I  have  other  good  news.  Today  I  have
authorized  the  kitchen  to  open  up  our
```

meat supplies. You will not be
disappointed. That is all."

A crowd gathers around the kitchen serving hatch.

"My lor'," says a woman at the head of the queue. She presses a food tray to her chest and stares at the meat.

"How much can I have?" she asks, wiping her lips.

"We have plenty," Sid says, "but let's be considerate to the other diners, everyone's hungry today." Sid takes a wide serving spoon and sinks it into the meat, hitting the bottom of the large silver dish with a clink. He serves a portion of meat onto her plate as a hungry line shuffle behind her. She carries away her food, displaying it to the crowd with a pantomime lick of her lips.

The impatient line mutters.

"Don't worry, I have more cooking in the kitchen," Sid says, easing the crowd's latent ire.

Next in line is Easter and baby, both swaddled in red.

"Hey! Here's my little lady and my big strong man!" Sid blooms over Easter and baby Quincy. He smiles and holds the child's hands, lifting the tiny palms so it looks like baby is celebrating a victory. Sid's weather-beaten cheeks crease with a smile, and he rests a gentle hand on Easter's shoulder and leans in for a kiss before serving more food.

People hustle and bustle to seats with full plates, dragging out chairs and clanking their cutlery.

"What kind of meat is it?" asks Drew, watching the juices run down the chins of gnashing and gnawing faces. Full mouths leer back at him.

"Someone said pork, but it's not. I think it's more like chicken," Hazel says.

"Oh…" Drew prods at his broiled meat with a fork.

"You're not eating yours?" Hazel says.

"Nah… first rule of the road. Well, second, actually. Never eat the mystery meat." He slides his plate towards her. "Maybe I'll get some rice, peas, and carrots, there's loads left." He glances towards a tray of rice and vegetables sitting untouched under a hot lamp beside the glistening meat.

"So, what's the first rule?" asks Hazel.

"Of what?"

"The road," she says, mid-chew.

"Oh, yeah, rule one of the road – Never poo in the bus toilet; the plumbing can't handle it."

She shakes her head. "I knew I'd regret asking." She smiles, glances at Drew, and laughs. He laughs back.

Eight people in blue gowns sit at the far end of the dining area and hand out work duties. Courtney's first in that particular line, and she's been assigned to the housekeeping crew by Oscar, who now wears the powerful powder blue.

"Excuse me, I'd prefer to work in the kitchen," Courtney says, "not that I mind the housekeeping duties, but I was a chef, and I think I have some skills to offer in the kitchen." In her flowing red gown, Courtney stands like a rose. Its color adds warmth to her cherry-red lips and her silver-gray eyes.

Peering over to the kitchen, Oscar calls out. "Hey, Sid, what do you think? She's got kitchen experience…" Oscar points to Courtney as a farmhand might to a cow.

Sid peaks out of the serving hatch and nods. "Sure, if she can chop carrots, she can start tomorrow."

Courtney's knees feel heavy, her balance becomes unsteady, and her breath becomes shallow. Nervous and isolated, she turns away from Sid and falls silent.

Does he recognize me? Does he care? Have patience… Choose the right time. His time will come…

31

BEDTIME

Another day passes as the night closes in, and Hazel's spent most of it trying to source a sliver of cell service. With her phone in her hand, she divined a route across every square inch of Salvation, checking and rechecking, until her crisscrossing raised some eyebrows.

"Don't be making problems like yo' friend Drew," Charlie says, but the comment didn't register. Instead, she recalls dancing with Drew.

What a terrible dancer...

Her lips curl to a smile, but it's made weak by the memory of all the disapproving faces staring at her and Drew in the Common Room. It's weakened more by her recollections of the Pastor's mania in the Sermon Hall, and it fades completely with the idea that tomorrow, she must endure another day in this place.

Despite being one day closer to the end of the hurricane, she feels tomorrow can bring her no good thing. Only dread and worry, swollen by the fear of hidden forces not yet revealed. At this late low point, she slumps on her bed with both the battery of her phone and her personal resolve running low.

"What's that you got, dear?" Barbara, Hazel's roommate, asks.

"My cell phone," she responds without looking up from the screen's glow.

Swipe down > airplane mode > on / off > wait... Still no signal. Kill all apps > Power off / Power on > try to make a call > make an emergency call. Nothing.

"Your cell phone, again," Barbara says plainly. "Is there somebody you want to call, dear?"

"Yes. Are there any windows at all in this place? Or stairs? Or a landline?" The last idea brightens Hazel, as if remembering an old friend.

"I don't know, dear. Sid knows a lot about this place. He helped set it up. Why don't you ask Sid? He helped Father set it up, him and the other lady. Sid is the one to talk to." Barbara thinks in circles, and it makes Hazel wince.

"Barbara?" Hazel's voice pitches to a question, "Do you ever... I mean... are you...?"

"What's that, dear?"

"Are you *happy* here? With the Pastor? In this place?" She cranes her neck over her phone to gauge Barbara's reaction. Barbara blinks beneath spectacles so thick she looks like a seal behind a block of ice.

"I am very happy, thank you very much. Thank Father we are here. I am very happy. Thanks to Father." Her words are plastic. She sits with her hands on her thighs. Hazel breaks her gaze, turns off her phone, and slides it beneath her pillow. Barbara's watchful expression stays on Hazel, like a child waiting to be dismissed by a teacher.

"Have we only been here for two days? Feels longer. It's all starting to blur together," Hazel says.

"Two full days, and this is the third night, and every minute of it has been Heaven. Thank Father." Barbara is older than most and Hazel assumes she learned to thank Father long ago in better days when it was perhaps more apt.

The two look at one another from opposing beds. The room, like all the others, is a small concrete cube. The light from the ceiling is harsh but not quite strong enough to properly illuminate. Diagonal shadows smear across the walls, and here and there a few flecks of stone are embedded in the ceiling. They glint like glitter. Hazel strains to hear the outside world, for the sound of birdsong or traffic, but there's nothing.

I need to get away from here. I need this hurricane to be over with. Relax, just one more day and the hurricane will be gone. Just one more day and I'll be free of this place.

The lights go out with a clunk and Hazel fumbles into bed, but the silence of Salvation keeps her awake. So too do thoughts of the Staples Center, the radio interviews, the terrible coffee at work, her blank office décor, the girls and the sunshine, and California's usual blue. It lies just beyond these walls, and it's all being ripped apart by Hurricane Jason. She stares at the ceiling and lets the darkness hold her gaze.

32

WHERE FORCE RULES

Drew stares into the twisting, inescapable darkness. Submerged in the oppressive blind, his thoughts – usually swirling and uncollected – are hushed into a deathly quietude that carries him into a dreamless sleep.

An alarm starts blaring.

The lights come on.

There's movement in the corridor.

It can't be morning already.

The PA announces, on repeat:

```
"All must report to the Sermon Hall
immediately. No exceptions. That is
all."
```

It's too bright, too early, but he finds a reserve of energy and joins the crowd in the corridor.

"What's going on?" he asks.

"Some sort of emergency," someone says.

The Pastor waits in the Sermon Hall. His black gown flows over his body like a shimmering quilt. His chair is perched on top of a large box, and the pews are not set in their usual uniform rows. They now form a semi-circle facing him and the blue-gowned Planning Committee who sit by his side. Without his usual fanfare, the Pastor speaks dispassionately to the gathered.

"There're some matters that we need to take care of – I've had several reports handed to me today. Troubling reports that some people are causing difficulties and we cannot have that here. We must cut all this out, so we're going to take care of it right now."

He scans a piece of paper handed to him by a Blue Gown and reads it aloud.

"Elsa Holt." His peeks over the note.

"It says here that on the first night Elsa was hostile. She did nothing to get on. In the morning, she claimed we're all liars. She has a nasty bad attitude. Talks back. Says she can't do this or that because of arthritis and cold. Grace Bell got mad and yelled at her. Elsa calls me Pastor and refuses to call me Dad or Father. She complains throughout the whole day."

He searches the crowd for Elsa and begins his cross-examination at a distance. "Why don't you get yourself together?"

Megan, in her blue gown, marches over, pulls Elsa up by the arm and pushes her into the middle of the semi-circle.

"Well, Father, I apologize," Elsa says, facing the Pastor. "I try my best. If you remember, we talked a time ago, and you said it was all right for me to call you Pastor."

He waves a hand. "No. We changed that. We passed a new law to get rid of all that talk, you just haven't been listening, have you? Listen – You call me either Dad or Father. No exceptions, no in-betweens. Got it?"

The crowd eye Elsa with a glassy, supercilious stare. Elsa's looks stirred but calm as she begins her defense. "Well, the man said–"

"I don't give a shit what the man said!" Father yells at full volume. "Since then, we changed the rules! Are you going to get your ass together? You can't be nasty! You can't be a smart assed! Why should we maintain an eighty-one-year-old woman who won't show proper gratitude or follow instructions or respect her father? Do you know how much your medications cost me? It costs more than your social security checks bring in, so from now on you call me *father*. That's the end of it. This is your last warning. Now be seated!"

He rubs his temples. Peering underneath the shadow of his hand he yells, "Charlie."

Wearing red, weighing in at 205 pounds and measuring six feet six inches, Charlie Hoya doesn't need Megan to lift him out of his seat. He stands on his own accord.

"Now, Charlie," Father reads from another scrap of paper, "here's the report – you've been argumentative. you have a bad attitude. Complaining constantly, arguing with the Planning Committee, asking people if they hate Dad, saying you're goin' to fight one person at a time and get out of here – Oh shit! You're a punk!"

The audience's shock feeds back into hate.

"Stop lettin' your pride keep you so busy," Father says. "Learn to cooperate and follow the rules!" He turns to the room and gestures, "He thinks he can leave and survive outside in the hurricane – he probably thinks he can even survive the Blue-eyed Monster – just one touch of the Blue Eye, Charlie, and…" Father skips lightly over his words. "How about that, O' Charlie-boy? Big ol' gangland Charlie-boy? How about the Blue-eye, Charlie-boy? How about the eye? How about the eye?"

The crowd enjoy the humor.

Father continues in his normal voice.

"We might as well be free from you. How about it, Charlie? You wanna touch the Blue-eye tonight? You got my blood pressure boiling – he can handle anything, he says. He can even handle the Monster – You punk! You wanna die? Do you, Charlie? I don't give a shit tonight."

"Look, Dad, um, I don't wanna die, but I ain't afraid to." Charlie rubs his shaven head. "Dad, like I said. I don't want to. Like I said, I was pissed at the time I said those things, but I feel like I shouldn't be on storeroom duty when I should be on the Planning Committee. I proved myself, and I don't think they told you right."

Megan breaks in. "No! No, Charlie! You just don't have a good attitude. What I don't understand is, if you're so goddam tough, why are you competing with us? Why don't you get on our side?" She looks to Father. "You know what Charlie said? He said he could fool us and play along. He won't be worthy until he cooperates and follows the rules. And you know what he said about you? He said you're a hustler – I've heard him say that, but his words don't manipulate me. I see him, and I see nothing but a glare of hate in his eyes."

The restless crowd break into a slow and rhythmic ululation.

Father cuts over the noise. "You ain't afraid to die, Charlie? I'd be ashamed to die if I was you." He throws his words like daggers. "Now everybody, get out of the way and let the Committee have him."

In a flash of blue, the Planning Committee surround Charlie, and the sound of Megan's fist smacking his nose elicits a chorus of "Woooooo" from the onlookers. The rest of the Blue Gowns attack and the dull fleshy impact of their blows elicit cheers from the crowd. They stand, jump and whoop, jostling Drew as bare knuckles rain down on Charlie. Charlie tries to swing, but he's forced to duck and shield from the ferocity and the sheer number of punches.

Charlie grunts and struggles. The attack is sustained and unrelenting, but there's one Blue Gown who is less animated than the others: Oscar. He steps from one foot to another, gesturing a forward movement, but never taking one.

"Oscar!" shouts Father. "Get involved! Get your ass in there!"

With an apologetic grimace, Oscar springs forward and strikes. His fists make full contact, not once, but several times in a devastating flurry of lefts and rights directly to Charlie's head.

"Come on, Charlie! Not so tough now!" Father smirks.

"I really do think he's had enough." says a trembling voice, almost inaudible above the noise of the shrill crowd. The Blue Gowns pause. The voice is Mother's.

"God dammit, why do you always take their side?" Father says. "You know, that could be misconstrued, the way you do that?" He turns back to Charlie. "Now somebody *get* that motherfucker!"

The Blue Gowns continue their work. Dull thumps, short full contact smacks, thwacks, and thuds land on their tense, tender target, and in the maelstrom of attack the Blue Gowns reach rhapsody.

Father lets the action run its course before he makes a final ruling.

"Back up, Megan. Back up a minute. Why do you do this, Charlie? I saved your ass from worse than death – the Los Angeles cops didn't make it easy with a gang record like yours. Why do you make it like this? Your toughness is doing nothing but making our lives a misery. You think that bravery is an end in itself. Let me tell you this, I've seen many heroes die. I have seen many heroes die for nothing at all. Bravery means shit unless it's connected to something.

"It's no good being gangland Charlie against the world. show me that you can be useful to our cause, show me that you can be a nice guy and make up for this hellish blood pressure tonight. I'm sick of it, there's no mercy in this place. I've suffered all night long. I hope you learn. I have to exert my power with a sense of justice because you stepped too far. When you are back in good health, I expect you to be on the job and doing your work with no problems."

Thick ribbons of blood fall from Charlie's nose. His eyes are split and swollen. Nurse Chamberlin and Sid drag him away, and the court is ready for its next defendant.

Reading from another fold of paper, Father moves on. "I have one last report about Drew. Drew Samuel. Oh, this motherfucker. Where is he? Bring him out here."

Drew had averted his gaze from Charlie's beating. In an act of conscious self-distraction, he forced his attention to escape the room.

Megan pulls him up by the arm and pushes him into the middle. He sees Hazel in the crowd with her hands over her mouth. The floor around Drew's feet is smattered with drops of Charlie's blood, some are messy and foot trodden, others are large, viscous pearls that glint in the light. The crowd on Drew's back is an intoxicated horde, wanting more.

"I see this report of Drew asking about the whereabouts of unknown people. Asking questions of everyone. Making people uncomfortable. Questionable motives. Generally, a little strange. All right. What the hell...?"

Drew heart races. He can't think of anything to say.

"All right. This is not our first run-in, is it, Drew? But this is your first time on the stand. Drew's been with us not even three days." Father looks at the Blue Gowns and waves the report. Anger rises from his chest. "What motherfucker wrote a report on someone who is so new to the damn Temple? Who decided that, instead of education, you'd have pieces torn off a new member who probably doesn't know the difference between right and wrong?"

The Blue Gowns look to the floor.

"Now, Drew, you *are* a motherfucker," Father says. "At least you've acted like one so far, and I don't care for strange questions and odd behavior. I don't know what in the hell is going through your mind, I really don't. You've got thought spaghetti, I never seen a man have it so bad. You might be crazy for all I know, but I'll give you some advice – get in line. Get on the team and step into it! Join the people. Join Salvation, and salvation shall be yours."

Drew stays silent but the hall has become a spirit in need of another sacrifice.

"Shave his head!" cries a voice. "Yeah!" yells another. "He oughta be punished! Shave his head!"

Father examines the evidence again. "OK, I see, you want to shave his head, right? Teach him a lesson that way? Well, as you know, we are not a democracy! I'm your father. Now sit down. I'm tired of this petty bullshit. This ain't no barbershop." He points a finger at Drew. "You'd be one of the best for our cause, if you'd get on the team and step in line. Listen to me. Don't give me no more trouble and start acting like you can be on the team. You could take a place by my side if you get yourself together. Or instead, you could go ahead and visit the barbershop, *and* the fuckin' Blue-eyed Monster for all I care. Now, sit down. And Drew, this is the last time I'm going to save your ass."

33

THE BAMBOO THAT BENDS IS STRONGER THAN THE OAK THAT RESISTS

Dismissed, the ireful crowd filters from the Sermon Hall and return to their beds, while Drew stands gazing down at his shadow, to where Charlie's blood stains the floor.

Poor Charlie should have just kept his head down and played along. There really is nowhere to hide in this place.

He walks back to his room to find it as humorless as he left it. The walls are cold, his bed is disheveled, and the dark and dirty ceiling seems darker and dirtier than before. As for the loudspeakers on the wall – the sight of those awkward trapezoid black boxes is one he's grown to particularly despise.

He looks at Tom's bed.

Was Tom real? I'm sure he was. What kind of spell has the Pastor cast on these freaks? What voodoo is this? How can he erase Tom's memory from all these people?

It's evident that fear is their keeper, and tonight Drew saw its power up close. He ponders fear and its strange bonding quality, its power to erase, its power to gather people, and its power to force community. With a heavy sigh, he gives up trying to find logic in this place. It just *is*, he decides, such is the power of fear.

Megan marches into the room and her blue gown shocks his senses.

"You think you're so special!" she says.

She pushes him against a wall by the neck and holds her face within biting distance of his face. Her teeth are clamped, her breathing is audible.

"You think you're better than us, don't you? Well, I see right through you. I see the way you look at us, and the way you look at Father. You're not better than us!"

She shouts something unintelligible and pushes his neck hard against the wall, and her nails press into his spine. He clenches his cheek and closes his eyes, feeling that a hard slap is, for whatever reason, surely due. The grip around his throat gets tighter. He opens his eyes as Megan presses a thumb into his windpipe and he feels the hard draw of restricted breath and pressure in the head. Her face is tense and expressionless. He closes his eyes again, certain he's about to pass out, and feels a strong, sudden pressure on his lips. Opening his eyes, he sees Megan up close, in the middle of a deep crushing kiss. She breaks away and slaps his face.

"I'm not sure I understand the rules here," he tries to say.

"You're a little bitch! You're nothing but meat to me and your time is gonna come. Do you understand me?!" She spits her words, and her cheeks flush a vicious shade. She withdraws her hand from around Drew's neck and pushes her forearm into his throat. "You like this, don't you?"

She reaches down and forces her hand up his gown. She takes his penis in her hand and squeezes it in a hate-filled grip. "Yeah, you like this, you sicko. This is what you want, isn't it? Yeah?" She's breathless. Faster and faster her hand moves, massaging him, more and more she leans on him, tightening her grip. "You little bitch. If I hear anymore bullshit from you, I'm going to snap this fucker off! Do you understand me?"

He nods, and her madness cools to indignation. Her teeth unclench, she removes her hand and releases Drew's throat as he slumps against the wall.

"Your time is gonna come." She storms out of the room and vanishes into darkness.

Drew takes a moment to wonder what is happening to him.

Maybe the Pastor right. I do I need to pick a team. Maybe life would be easier if I did.

The thought is comforting. It feels like the future.

The lights snap off.

34

I FEEL NO LIGHT INSIDE ME STRONG ENOUGH
TO RESIST THE DARK

The horrible night becomes a horrible morning, and once again, Hazel sits in the Common Room eating cold egg slush. To her left, Barbara scoops at her plate, and to her right, Easter and child have joined them in a collective silence.

Courtney will already be in the kitchen, I suppose.

She scans the room with her fork idling between her chin and her plate.

And where the hell is Drew? Come on, Drew.

"Who you waitin' on, child?" Barbara blows on her already-cold eggs.

"You remember," Hazel trails off, trying to find the words. "No one. Never mind…"

"Na', don't you worry. E'erthing gonna be all right for us." Barbara's stilted reassurance goes unnoticed by Hazel, who's only just rising out of the shadow of her mind to notice Easter and baby at her side. Feeling a prang of guilt for being impolite, she attempts some conversation.

"So, how's little Quincy, Easter? Are you well? You look good."

"Thank you," Easter says. "I still feel exhausted but I'm very happy. Look at my little Quincy. He's my everything now, and so precious. You know, me and Sid had been trying for ages."

"Yeah?"

"Yeah. We tried everything. We tried the medical route, the home remedy routes, believe me, you don't want to know. But then came Father, and he made it so we could have a baby. It's a miracle, isn't it?"

Hazel doesn't know quite how to respond, so she lets the moment pass like a fading breeze and leaves the table to scrape the remains of her breakfast into the trash. Megan, in her brazen blue, appears by her side.

"So, *Hazel*, isn't it?" Megan says. "I've been meaning to catch up with you. How are you?"

"Tripping on the vibes of life," Hazel says, wiping the mush off her plate with her knife.

"So, how are you finding Salvation?" Megan says, smiling.

"It's an experience."

"Oh really? What does that mean?"

"How would *you* explain it?" Hazel hears sharpness in her own voice.

"Well, I think it's paradise. Thank Father we are here, is all I can say. What do you think of Father? Do you see him as God? A prophet? Or do you see him as more of a Lenin figure? What do you think?"

There is nowhere to escape.

"He's the sum of the human condition," is all Hazel think of. It's nonsense and she knows it, but it is such a fine line of bullshit that it might stand half a chance of confusing Megan into silence. It succeeds, and Megan stands with narrowed eyes, contemplating the nonsense.

Two to three days, just remember. The hurricane will last no more than three days, that's what my data said.

The clink and clunk of knives and forks on plates squeak in the sparse morning atmosphere. After the dishes are cleared, the diners, weary from the episode of nocturnal justice, prepare for their day's work.

Hazel is to teach in the classroom, which has been prepared by the church for Salvation's youth, eleven years and under.

No Courtney, and no Drew. This breakfast sucks. She gives up the wait and goes to find the classroom. She doesn't know what the class is to be. She's been told all will become clear once she arrives at work.

The classroom is large, pretty, and decorated in primary colors. Children's paintings of families, houses, and shining suns decorate the walls. A projector hangs from the ceiling, its lens points at a patch of gray that's framed in yellow.

Hazel has developed a tic. Every few minutes she feels an urge to check her phone and observe its dwindling battery, and lack of signal. Her gown has no pockets, which makes this habit awkward. But walking around with a phone in her hand might cause someone to report her, so she's decided to smuggle the device around in the waistline of her underwear. It's not comfortable – and she has to ungracefully lift her gown to retrieve the phone, which she does quickly. Once in hand, she powers it on just long enough to check for a signal.

No bars. Damnit. And the battery's very low.

She walks around the classroom, holding the phone out at angles, until the sound of footsteps in the corridor disturbs her.

She swipes the phone off and returns it to her midriff just before the door opens and the Pastor walks in leading a troop of children. He looks like a giant leading a pack of red-robed dwarfs. Hazel counts twenty-seven young minds.

"Now, class, this is your teacher. Say hello to Miss Cox," Father says.

"Hello, Miss Cox." the children say in discordant unison. Each child smiles and instinctively sits on their tailbones, folding their arms and legs.

"I will lead the first class," Father says, "and I'll visit from time to time. But when I'm not around, Miss Cox will teach reading, writing, math and science. I will teach history. OK, kids? Does that sound like fun?"

"Yes, Father." drone the kids.

"OK, children. Look around at your new school. Isn't it wonderful? Yes, education, education, education." He towers over them. "We can overcome a great many challenges with learning. This place will be where you develop your talents, raise your ambitions and make Salvation fairer and stronger. This place will be where you gain the basic tools for life and work. You will learn the joy of life, the satisfaction of math, the beauty of art, the magic of science, and the purity of truth."

The children, all with mop-top haircuts, some with itchy noses, and most with restless wriggles, smile at Father with shiny, puffy cheeks and tiny teeth.

"Today's lesson is a very important one from history. I'm going to show you all a movie. You all like movies, don't you, kids?" Father doesn't let them answer. "Today is a special movie. You have heard me talk about false gods. Well, this movie is about the false gods of money and the old society. This movie will show you just what they wanted to do to you. This is what they had planned for you all. So, as you watch, remember this is what was waiting for you, and for your families until Father saved you."

He fires up the projector, and a faded blue trapezoid appears on the wall opposite. The blue deepens and morphs into a dark image and a grainy black and white title appears. It reads "The Holocaust of the Jews".

For twenty soundless minutes, images of skin pulled tight over bone cover the wall. Crowds of living skeletons stare at the children from behind barbed wire. Desperate faces tower over the little minds. Pictures showing piles of bodies cause some children to look at their feet. Some cry and sniffle.

Father stops the playback.

"Now, I saw you look away, Julie-May. We're going to watch that again, and this time everybody watches. It's important that we all know about this. This is what they were going to do to you – to your mother, your father, until you were saved."

And the reel runs again, but Hazel doesn't notice the ghostly light dancing on the wall the second time. The silence gives her a moment to consider the outside world, and how Hurricane Jason must be at its worst point by now. It will be leveling the land, ripping up houses by the roots, carrying off cattle by the herd, twisting and flattening pylons to lift and choke the dusty sky. But in Hazel's mind, her California still exists. Her favorite beer garden still out there – as is her is office, and Lara, Sissy and Sunday afternoons. Even Flynn is there, sitting on her desk, waiting for her in the office. In her mind's eye, they all still exist exactly as they were. But in reality, she can't be sure, and it wearies her to despair.

After the distortion of recent events: the hurricane, the red gowns, the concrete walls, a flash of freak rationality enters her mind. She can't just ask Father to let her leave, and she knows she can't just walk out of here. If she asks, she'll likely end up missing like Tom or beaten like Charlie. She sees the tortured bodies on the wall, the tortured souls. She thinks about the Nazis, of Hitler, and of that singular moment when he turned a gun on himself as an act of escape. And how the Third Reich fell soon after. She looks at Father and considers what might have to be done.

"Stop that! Stop that!" Father leaps to his feet and dashes to the side of a young boy.

"That bug wasn't hurting you!"

Hazel stops the movie, and Father adopts a new tone.

"I saw you. Don't you tell me you weren't. I saw you step your foot on that bug and play with its wings. That's not fair and that's not right. You dissect things in biology class, out of necessity, when they're dead. Why did you do it? Why did you kill it?"

The child offers no explanation, so Father turns to Hazel. "Can you set up some counseling for these kids? We got a kid like this, so please set up some counseling in the teaching program." He turns back to the child, "I'm going to give you a break this time, 'coz teacher will put you into a class, and you can talk about why you stepped on that bug. Do you understand what I'm saying? Don't torture things. The world is so full of pain, and that poor bug was still alive when you finished. Did you tear his wing off? I'm sick of kids doing this. Hazel, if I'm overreacting, you tell me."

"…No," Hazel says.

Father continues, "If you don't learn sensitivity for life as a child, you sure aren't going to learn it later. I can't even eat chicken I've seen so many of them die. They can tell what's going to happen to them. It's not anthropomorphic, they can tell. I don't like brutality unless it's necessary. It tears the hell out of me."

Father leaves the children in Hazel's sole command. Numbed by Father's teachings, she searches her mind for a way to occupy twenty-seven students. Throwing her mind back twenty years to her own school days, she draws a vague plan of how to waste what remains of the day. She gathers the little red gnomes in a circle on the floor and has them introduce themselves.

"Now everyone, please introduce yourself to the group with your name, and tell us a little something about you," she instructs the class in what she hopes will be a very low impact end to her day's duties.

"Hello everyone. My name is Walter," says the first bright young boy. "I am eleven, and I am a I'm a violent revo... a violent revolution-ship." He looks around, "Is that right?"

The class giggles, the littlest of them laughs so hard he falls over. One child says, "No! It's 'revolutionary', dummy!"

"What do you mean?" Hazel is perplexed by the child, and uncomfortable by the cold floor.

"I mean I am a violent revolutionary," the child says.

"Do you know what that means?" Hazel asks.

"It means that the capital, capitalistic people, um, that way we can... I would like to, er, overthrow this country right now."

The words trigger a transient flush of alarm. She asks the boy, "Is that right?"

"We all are violent revolutionaries," says another youth. Other children nod and agree.

Astonished, Hazel asks, "What are you fighting against?"

The boys and girls look uncomfortable, and with no warning, Hazel slumps into a crippling, stress induced mental fatigue. The unreality of the moment, and of the many moments before it collect and strike her as if they were equal to years. This place and these conditions suddenly bear down on her like a dead weight, and weariness sets in deep, as if her brain is in the process of shutting down. Catching herself in a yawn she asks, "Who taught you to say those words?"

"Father," they say.

Her tired mind turns back to escape, but her thoughts have wandered into a thick gray fog. With another yawn, she strains to focus on the only genuine plan she has.

Courtney, you better get those damn keys.

35

THE AXE FORGETS, BUT THE TREE REMEMBERS

There's no time to sit and relax underneath Salvation's concrete curtain, everyone must work. The housekeepers, the laundry crew, the storeroom, sewing circle and the repair personnel are all busy. While in private rooms, the Planning Committee gather and consider before spreading out to monitor Salvation's good work.

If you were dressed in a blue gown and were free to roam the corridors of the shelter, you'd feel the cold concrete floor through the soles of your shoes as you walk a dimly lit, musty corridor. You'd probably follow your nose to the better fragranced air of the kitchen, where, by the better light of that place, you'd see Courtney and Sid coming face to face for the first time.

Sid begins her induction. "The first rule – don't go in the freezer, OK? After the shift is over, the freezer gets locked by me. I got the key here." He pats his waist and reveals a glinting ring of keys.

"Second rule," he continues, "smile and you'll be fine." He pats her on the back and walks to the rear counter, not noticing her flinch.

Her nerves are getting the better of her. Anger and fear have become two moons pushing and pulling the tide of her mind, but her thoughts always return to the same question: how insignificant must Sid's murderous actions have been in his own mind? So small and inconsequential, the act of destroying her life, that he doesn't remember her at all. At the time of Ethan's death, Sid didn't even pause to acknowledge her heartbreak on the blood-soaked checkout floor. Trembling, she fixes her eyes on the view through the serving hatch, to the Common Room, where Easter sits rocking little Quincy while several other women make a happy fuss over the young boy.

Such a shame. This is going to cause such a commotion...

She looks away and surveys the kitchen.

The kitchen is about twice the size of her sleeping quarters. Scratched steel work surfaces stretch the length of two walls – one behind her, where Sid is running water into a sink; and one in front, which features the serving hatch and a small chopping board. To her right is a gas-fired stove. To her left is a large walk-in freezer, which dominates the space. Its entrance is a huge, frosted metal door.

An ideal place to hide a body.

Sid leans over her shoulder and slaps a knife on the chopping board. She feels his breath on her face.

"Chop the carrots for tonight's meal. I've a pot boiling already." He lifts the lid of a tall stainless-steel pot, releasing a cloud of steam and frantic bubbles on frothing water. He kisses his fingers. "Good, honest food."

The heat of the kitchen is heavy on her brow. A large pile of washed carrots sits on the countertop near the chopping board. She picks up the cold knife. It's heavy, with a deep ridged crescent blade above a black plastic handle. A fine tool for its purpose.

"Go ahead, do your worst," he says, with an encouraging smile.

Courtney's mind spins.

Pick the right moment.

Looking out from the serving hatch, she glances at Easter and Quincy. She slowly chops the carrots, watching Easter laugh, smile, and play with her child. The fibrous break and muted clop of the knife on the cutting board distracts her as she struggles between two worlds.

She remembers Ethan so clearly, and so vividly she remembers the good times. They were always good times: the vacations to the Maldives, the scattering fish; his face in the snorkel, his laughter. Now he's gone, for no reason at all. So unnecessary, so unfair. He's gone forever, and the man who took him away stands beside her and she has a knife in her hand.

Now.

Her heart flutters, her nerves splinter, and her adrenaline pulses. She reaches bursting point.

"Hey, are you OK?" Sid looks at her with a breed of concern that could be mistaken for frustration. He taps her shoulder, less attentive than earlier. She turns to and face him, holding the knife at her back as if it might confess her murderous thoughts.

"Hey, don't worry, Courtney. Everything's going to be A-OK, all right?" He places his hand on her arm and feels her tremble. Her chest moves with quick breathing, her skin feels flushed. Sid stares. There's a flicker of recognition his eyes.

"Oh! You! Oh no, oh no! Not the lady from the supermarket. Oh, my God. I'm sorry, I'm so sorry…"

He turns his back briefly, too quick for Courtney to act.

He turns to her again and, looking in her eyes, says, "I'm so sorry."

Her body relaxes a little, the last syllable of his last word hangs in the air as he steps closer and plunges a knife deep into her abdomen.

Shock fires through her body, her muscles ripple and tighten. With sharp breaths, her eyes grow wide, and she looks down to see a slender black handle protruding from her stomach. At its base, surrounded by a dark red growing plume, is the silvery shimmer of the blade's heel against the blood-soaked red gown. Fragments of light swirl. She falls to the floor.

Sid grabs her by the hair and drags her to the freezer.

"I'm sorry it had to be this way," he says, "but I can hardly trust a lady with a knife when she's got that look in her eyes – not in this place. It's better this way. It was always going to be this way. I'm so sorry."

He swings the freezer door open and a crest of white vapor swims over her. Blood streams out of her wound and red drops fall from her lips, she tries to pull the knife out, but her strength is evaporating, the light is fading, her breath is slipping. She desperately tries to crawl along the floor towards the exit, but Sid stops her with a boot on her back, pushing the knife in deeper and drags her back to the freezer.

She stares into the cold void of the refrigerator, gazing back from within looms a stiff unflinching figure. To her failing, panicking, dying mind, it appears to be the Grim Reaper coming to steal her away. But this is no reaper. Above her is the frozen specter of Tom, suspended on a hook lodged into his back. The vision transforms from reaper to sacrifice in an instant.

Tom's face fixed with the expression of a boy begging for his life, but no mercy came to him. His skin is marbled blue, his lips are frozen black. His veins, filled with iced blood, have risen to the surface and formed a thick network of ridges protruding from his thin, contracted skin. All that remains is a head and a limbless torso, and smears of thick chilled blood stain his body and gives testament to the torture he had endured. His last mortal moments of terror and are frozen on his face: his eyes are deeply buried under fiercely closed bruised lids that have wrinkled and frosted crystal white. Mist rises from his open mouth, his sparkling shoulders, and his frost-tipped hair.

Courtney's body is limp, and the light of her mortal world grows dim. Sid picks her up and throws her into the freezer beneath Tom's corpse. A few drops of cold blood drip from his four-times amputated body, and she gasps for air in the bitter cold space. The brightness of the kitchen narrows as the door closes, and a glacial blanket envelops as her broken heart beats its last.

36

A DROP OF LOVE

The day draws to its afternoon and a fine daffodil yellow figure floats through the gray corridors. She waves and smiles into rooms full of hard-working people as she passes.

Her steps stop at the entrance of the medical bay.

She unlocks the door and steps inside.

Stephen lies on one bed, sleeping. Charlie sits in another – no longer dressed in Salvation red, his new gown is hospital white. Mother, in her fine summer gown takes a seat beside him, wipes his brow and inspects his injuries.

"Oh, my poor child. I'm so sorry," she says.

"It's OK, Mom. I gave them some too. This is just how it is. I heard you call for me, though. I know you tried, and I appreciate it. But you didn't need to." He lifts his head and tips a cup of water to the less swollen side of his mouth. He swallows hard and lies back on his pillow. Mother takes his hand. With a shake of her head, she looks at his bruised swollen eyes and torn lips.

"Father is Father." she says in a whisper. It's all she can muster. "And Father does love you," she adds.

She feels she's aged a decade in the last few days.

"I love him too. He just don't see it," Charlie says, "I wanna make you both proud, Momma."

Father's voice slurs through the loudspeakers. She winces at the words in an effort to make sense of what he's saying:

> "One day will come. One day when the storm passes… when it is very safe… we will go out into the world. You will find it very much changed. Very much changed… changed. There are likely to be survivors. You should not approach them. Anybody you see might kill you. Do not think they would interpret you as a friend, no matter who they are or what they say… they are extremely paranoid, they are very vicious and are filled with raging hate from guilt. They dream nightly… dream nightly… and to the last of them, they have tremendous guilt… they are plotting against us, to invade us. They have tremendous guilt… be vigilant… be very, very vigilant."

Father begins his speech again in the same slurred manner, as if stuck in a loop, and the third time, he trails off as if he were slipping into an unwilling sleep.

"Momma, can I ask you a question?" Charlie says.

"Of course."

"Did you know Father was special when you first met him?"

She smiles softly. "Oh, no. Back then he was only sixteen. He came into my mother's flower store to buy some lilies – his own mother had just got out of hospital after being very sick.

After the first day, he kept coming in and buying flowers every day for what must have been a week. He must have spent a small fortune.

"I later learned that he didn't need all those extra flowers. He just kept coming in to ask me out to dinner, but he was so shy, so sweet. Every time he came to the counter to ask me out, he would lose his nerve and end up buying whatever flowers were within arm's reach. One day he ended up buying the biggest, most expensive bouquet because it was the only thing at the counter. He went pale when I rang it up, but he bought it anyway.

"I asked him, 'Do you want me to write a card for the flowers?' He didn't know what to say, so he just nodded. I asked him what he wanted me to write. He said, 'Can you write, from Quincy.'"

"I asked if that was the whole message, and he got red in the face and said, 'Would you go out to dinner with me tonight?' So, I wrote that on the card! Then I said, 'Who should I make the card out to?' And he looked at me with a funny smile and said, 'To Anna' – that's my name – so, I wrote that down, too. I read it back to myself and said, 'Yes, I'd love to.'

"That was way before he started preaching. As time wore on, he took a job as an apprentice preacher, and he preached the gospel like no one else. It was good and success came easy to him. His star rose and we'd would go to dinner parties with politicians and make TV and radio appearances together. We were the toast of California in those days. Then something must have happened, but I don't know what, or when. Even when it happens up close, it's hard to see change – especially when it's slow, and especially when it's something you don't want to see.

Maybe you can forgive too much, I don't know, now, all these years later..."

She let's go of Charlie's hand and frets with the hem of her gown. There's no clock in the room, no pictures, no TV, no radio, and no window to gaze out of. The old world had indeed been swept away.

"Charlie, we might as well be at the bottom of the sea for all this place is. Is this the price we pay for salvation? What is a life when it's wrapped in concrete? Sometimes... I'm sure these walls are getting smaller."

Her thoughts swim away and Charlie drifts into sleep.

37

ALL EYES GRADUALLY ADJUST TO THE DARKNESS

Drew rose early this morning. He passed on breakfast, and headed straight to the laundry room, where he found a mound of bed sheets and dirty towels waiting for him. The towels on top of the heap are stained blood red.

Must be Charlie's blood.

The Planning Committee made a mess of Charlie last night, but even so, it seems like a lot of red to clean – which is unfortunate for Drew, because by the grace of God, there are no washing machines in Salvation. He has to pummel the stains out by hand in a large trough filled with cold water from a hose. The water runs red on contact with the towels, and blood is a stubborn stain. It's not long before Drew's hands are wrinkled and sore.

Working alongside him are twin brothers, Nick and Rod. Together, they push and knead the towels.

"Hey, Drew, remove your watch or it'll break in the water," Nick says.

"It's broken anyway. It got drenched in the storm before we arrived. Look at that – 7:11. Must've been the time we got here."

"You know ol' Ollie fixes watches in the workshop, right?" Rod says.

"I didn't know that. How much does he charge? I haven't got any money with me."

Rod shakes his head and laughs. "You really are new around here, aren't you? No cost, man. Just take it to him and he'll fix it."

The workshop is in the bowels of Salvation. It consists of two men working at two desks in the middle of a room full of salvage material. There are boxes containing a history of broken domestic appliances: vacuum cleaners, clock parts, one is full of irons, another is full of hair dryers, and several brim with broken blenders. On one shelf, next to a pile of snapped spectacles, is a small collection of broken wristwatches. Always finding some redeeming value in even the most broken of objects, the two men appear to throw nothing away, and they stay busy giving new life to various smashed, bent and poorly used things. The older of the two is working on a bass guitar, presumably for the band. Its red body lies in front of him with its scratch plate open. He holds a soldering iron to its belly while a young man sits opposite, trying to straighten a pair of eyeglasses.

"You finished that broom yet, kid?" says the elder.

"Does this look like a broom to you?"

"Fine, fine. But when your sister comes in here looking for her broom and it's not fixed, I'm going to tell her it's your ass she needs to whoop."

"She got no chance of whooping my ass without these glasses I'm fixing for her."

"She don't need glasses to see your ugly ass. How'd she break her glasses and her broom at the same time, anyway? Playing Quidditch?"

"Hey, fellas," Drew says.

"Hey. Drew, is it?" the older man says, "Come on in and save me from having to talk to this fool."

"You Ollie?"

"That's me. That a watch in your hand?"

"It got wet," Drew looks at his waterlogged Polex.

"Not a problem. I'll get to it later today. Unless I gotta fix a broom in a hurry."

"Thanks, Ollie."

"Oh, Drew," Ollie says.

"Yeah?"

"You know, we don't charge money around here, but on this occasion, I'd like to trade something with you. There's one thing you can do for me in return for fixin' this watch."

"Yeah?"

"Yeah. The one thing you can do for me. Well, I guess it's two things really – relax and be at peace. Can you do those things for me?"

"I think I can do that." Drew nods and waves goodbye, but he stops. "Nice Hofner you got there by the way." He gestures to the bass in front of Ollie.

"It sure is." Ollie smiles.

"What's up with it?"

"This guitar? You know, this thing here is a little like you. It's known for its quirks, but all it needs is a little care and attention an' it'll be just fine."

Drew returns to the laundry room and settles into punching the stains out of the towels. Through the thumping, kneading and cleaning, the movie reel of his life plays back in high emotional resolution. Flashes of Charlie's beating rush in, interspersed with memories of tour buses, stages, hotels and airplanes, marking them all with the same dreadful feeling he felt when Father called his name last night.

Maybe I should cut my hair after all, he wonders.

The evening enters the narrow phase of day when people's time becomes their own. Evenings used mean high stress for Drew because they used to mean Show Time. But no longer. After his work is done, he heads to his sleeping quarters with a damp towel slung over his shoulder. On the way to his room, he waves hello to Barbara, who's sitting at a table, deep in a game of patience, and he says hi to Karis, who's sketching a charcoal portrait of Father. The common room is full of people enjoying their leisure time with carefree smiles, while children play pat-a-cake and skip and laugh in the corridor. Loud yells come from one room, where Florence has gathered four other girls with the intention of forming the first ever dance group in the history of Salvation. "...Five, six, seven, eight and step!" He stops and encourages with positive words, then heads to the sewing room to borrow a pair of scissors from Darlene.

38

SOFT HANDS, HARD WORDS

Drew's makeshift barbershop is almost complete. He has a towel big enough to wrap around his shoulders, scissors sharp enough for the job, and he's in possession of some hard-earned leisure time. But his barbershop is missing a barber.

"Hazel! Come here! Come cut my hair." He grabs her wrist and hurries her into his room. "You saw what they said last night. The buggers want to cut my hair, so I'll do the work for them." He smiles. "You can tell me about your day while you cut."

"My day? I spent most of it teaching children about the Holocaust," she says, grimacing. "Your day been any better?"

"I spent the day punching blood out of towels."

"Fabulous!"

They laugh in mild madness.

Hazel perches on the bed, while Drew sits on the floor in front of her.

"What makes you think I can cut hair, anyway?" she says. "I used to cut my ex-boyfriend's hair, but that was a long time ago. He had fairer hair, thinner than yours. Yours is nice. You're definitely sure about this?"

"Go for it."

The snip-snap of scissors chime above his head as Hazel cuts in rough measures.

"OK. Turn and look at me, I want to check the sides." Drew doesn't respond. "Drew?" She slaps him on the head.

"Oh, you finished?" He faces her, wiping lose hair from his neck. "That was quick. You didn't have to rush."

"I'm not finished. I need to see if the sides are even." She casts her eyes from ear to ear with his hair between her fingertips.

"Drew," she whispers. "Drew!"

"Yeah."

"The band sounds good tonight, don't they? I can hear them down the corridor."

Drew looks at the corridor, nodding in more-or-less approval. "I suppose."

"Drew, the band isn't playing tonight. It's their night off."

"Ah."

"You struggle to hear, don't you?"

"My ears aren't what they were – ruptured eardrums. I need surgery to repair them, apparently. It's about eight grand per ear, so I'm waiting for the tour money to come through."

"So, you've seen a doctor already?" she says, exaggerating her words.

"You don't need to pantomime for my benefit. I've gotten this far, so speak normally. As long as I can see your lips move, we're good. But, yeah, saw a doctor when my hearing went south. I drank myself into a pretty bad state first though, and I don't remember much about it – only that I woke up in hospital in Berlin. I'd lost my phone, my wallet, and my passport. The tour couldn't find me, so they went to the next show without me – to do what, I don't know. I was the talent. Anyway, imagine waking up in a hospital in Germany with no recollection of how you got there, and you can't hear a thing.

"They brought in a translator, and through her I asked the doctor about my hearing. He sent me to the audiology department and put me through the usual tests – you know, where they tell you what frequencies you can and can't hear. It was kind of a waste of time, I already knew what I couldn't hear. They did more exams and told me I need to have my ear drums surgically repaired, and that news pretty much ended my DJ career."

"I'm sorry."

"It's fine. Life's just hard sometimes."

"It certainly feels that way right now. Just look where we are, and who we're with!"

"These people aren't that bad, you know? There's some nice people here."

"Maybe, but I can't understand why they follow the Pastor. They must all be crazy to believe in him."

Drew shrugs. "I don't think they all *believe* him. They just follow him because they have nothing else. Believing and following are two different things. You don't need one to have the other."

"Either way, they're all nuts for all I care." Hazel ruffles his hair.

"I don't blame them really," he says.

"Of course, you do. The things he says are insane. The things he does are insane. I mean, who is this guy? I can't believe anyone would listen to him."

Drew runs a hand through his new, shorter hair style. "I remember when I was about six or seven, I was fighting with my older brother in the yard, and we went rolling around on the grass. We rolled one way and then another. Then, bang! I smashed my head on a manhole cover. It hurt like hell, and I remember crying and crying, and I had this massive headache. After a visit to the hospital, I spent the rest of the day on the couch in my mum's arms, and when I was curled up by her side, I didn't have a care in the world because she was there. I don't remember any pain and I felt safe – like nothing could get to me through her." He shook his head. "Don't you miss that feeling of being cared for? Being protected? I think as we get older, we forget about the time when we had someone we could trust like that. What if there was someone who could take away all the stress, all the pain, and shelter you. Because let's be honest, life's too hard and we're all just left to fend for ourselves. We could all do with a little help, and I'd happily let someone else take the wheel for a while. But there aren't exactly many people willing to take on the job, so if there's somebody willing to take care of all the hassle, who cares if he's a little nuts?"

"Are you crazy? That's called dependence, and you give all that up when you become an adult, remember? It's a natural process called growing up. Independence is the whole point of being an adult. I can't believe I have to explain this to you."

"I don't know," he concedes.

"Well, I do. There's nothing wrong with having faith or looking to someone or something for strength, but that's not what's going on here. It could be that some of these people came to the Pastor genuinely searching for something positive, but at some point, he bullshitted them, and they went along with it, and let him pervert their ideas. They might say they don't really believe him or even agree with him, but that's no excuse for enabling him. They let this Pastor have total power over them, and once you give that up it's hard to get back. My guess is these people just want a simple life. Simple rules and a pat on the head from Daddy." She shakes her head. "But that's not what life is about. Life's about living and growing on your own terms and meeting the struggle head on. An easy life – that's his appeal, but it's all bullshit. He exploits people's vulnerabilities." She dusts the loose hair from his shoulders.

"Easy?" Drew says, picking on that one word. "Why does life have to be hard? And what good does independence and responsibility bring you if all they equate to is struggle? All people want in life is happiness, and that shouldn't be so hard to find – it should be built in. A simple purpose should be all that we need. And we should get it. Instead, life demands so much from us, and we get pushed and pulled at all angles." He pauses. "We have the media scaring the pants off us every day. Then we get sent out into the rat race and we start to believe that we *need* things, just to feel better – a bigger car, a bigger house, technology, *likes*. And the world will let you have everything if you can afford it. But that's not happiness. What happens when you're working two or three jobs and you're still not able to pay the rent, and you haven't seen your family in months? Life stretches people to breaking point, and then it keeps stretching. Why are basic things, like happiness, the hardest to get? Has it been that way for every generation, or did we just fuck it up?"

"It depends on your point of view," she says, sighing. "For some, life is hard and for some it's not, but ultimately it's all in your mind. Some people don't know what to do with the freedom, the choices, and the overall uncertainty of life. These people need simple rules, so they feel like it all makes sense. While other don't shy away from the challenges and the decisions. While some use life to express themselves, others need a patriarch – someone to follow, someone to please, someone to tell them they're special, someone to make it simple, a buffer between them and real life. That's what this place is. A buffer between these people and reality."

"Is that a bad thing?" he says. "I can see the appeal. What if life could be easy? I'm in my thirties and it's only getting harder. What if you could let somebody else bother with the work, the worries, the decisions, the survival, the future, the fuckups, and the wasted time."

She eyes him sideways. "You sound like one of them. You're better than this, you can do better than hide behind someone else. Life is about the decisions *you* make, not the ones you let someone else make for you. Life can be whatever you want it to be, it can be bliss or it can be hell. It can be simple, or it can be complicated – or both. It's your choice. And it doesn't matter how old you are, and it doesn't matter how many fuckups you've made, or how much time you've wasted, because right now is the only moment you've got. So make the most of it." She takes his hand. "And Drew, right now I need you right here with me."

She stares into his eyes.

"Maybe." he says, mulling it over. "Thinking about it, if you're right and we all need to make the most of the moment, there's really only one thing we can do."

He leans forward and they come together as if draw by an invisible thread. The bloom of soft lips and the rush of new, delicate excitement send his pulse racing.

The loudspeaker comes to life:

```
"Would the following people immediately
report to the Sermon Hall. All members
of   the   Planning   Committee,   plus
Bethany, Aiden, his family, and Drew
Samuel. That is all."
```

"Drew, Father – *shit*, I mean, the Pastor just called for you over the PA. He wants you and the Planning Committee to go to the Sermon Hall right now. This can't be good. We need to get out of here. I'm scared of this place, and I'm worried we're going to be trapped in here forever."

"Don't worry. Here's what we do – I'll go to this meeting while you go and find Courtney and get the keys. Afterwards, we'll meet and get out of here. Till then, let's just play along and stay safe."

39

TOWN MEETING

"You must all be prepared," the Pastor says, "because a father who truly loves you prepares for all things. So, please understand, we must all be ready for such an occasion." His high seat has become a permanent fixture inside the Sermon Hall. Nurse Chamberlin clutches a pen and a notepad, which give her a secretarial air.

The Pastor continues. "One day we may have the United States military banging on our door with their top rank begging to get in to take shelter. What we have here is a desirable place – make no doubt about that. There will be a handful of survivors out there who will come scavenging. They will seek higher ground, and they will find us. And they'll come to take what we have. The people who will come here will try to harm us. They're peddlers of hate." He looks around the room. "Does anybody have any contribution to make on that point?"

Aiden, a slender man with a wisp of blond hair and piercing blue eyes, stands.

"Dad, in 2003 to 2006 the United States sent me to Iraq to fight a war I didn't know anything about. Since I joined the Temple, you've saved my life many times. Now I'm living with you, I'm living on your time, and if people come and try to take what we have, I'll fight. I would die for you right now, Dad. I'm willing to face the front line with you. Thank you."

Applause smatters the walls of the almost empty room while Nurse Chamberlin writes in her notepad.

"It's no great mumble," the Pastor says. "One must plan for one's own death. We must have a plan because we do not want to leave things to chance. To die without a plan would be a mistake you can't take back. We're born crying, but we should die in celebration. Bethany, what do you say?"

"Well, Dad, ever since I've been here, all I've seen is the beauty of Salvation. You all are my family, and I feel that my life is fulfilled. And if death comes it's no big deal to me, because I've already lived my life just being here with the family and I'd fight for that."

A clap of hands.

A small child, Aiden's daughter, rises to her feet. "I'm prepared to die for this family if I have to. Thank you, Dad."

Megan stirs. "Yeah, you'd die, but would you *fight*?"

"Now, hold on," the Pastor says, "Megan has brought up a sensitive question, and you may not understand the gravity of it. All children must face this – you must have no difficulty in facing this kind of thought."

Megan addresses Aiden. "Aiden, you've been good to us. I know you have your legal training, and your judgement has been invaluable to the Temple all these years. So, what do you say? Here's a question – if the State were coming up the road right now and we were gonna lay down our lives and fight, you say you would fight and give your life. But would you leave your daughter for the invader to have? What would you do in that case?"

Aiden rubs his chin. His eyes tick over the question.

"If it came to that, I would have to take her life."

Mutters of "Yes", and "Exactly right", underline the point.

"That's fine, Aiden. But she's old enough, she'll fight. How old is your child?" asks the Pastor.

"She's eleven."

"We fight at eleven," the Pastor says. "She'd take up a knife and she'd fight until she was dead. Unless it came to an overwhelming invasion. Then we would gently send her to sleep. We're already prepared for that. People who are really loving and genuinely compassionate prepare for such emergencies. Martin Luther King wrote, 'We must develop the quiet dignity of dying for our cause', and we likewise affirm that. Before we will submit quietly, we will resist actively, and put our lives on the line, if it comes to it. We've chosen our model. We will not march into the gas ovens. We will fight like those in the Warsaw ghetto. Patrick Henry said it best, 'Give me liberty or give me death'. And if people cannot appreciate a willingness to die for an uncompromised right to exist free from harassment, then they will never understand the integrity, the bravery and the honesty of this movement or the depth of commitment your father has to his principles. Drew, what do you say?"

Under the heat of attention, Drew's resolve evaporates like desert snow.

"I'd fight for what I believe in."

A flash of suspicion twists Nurse Chamberlin's face, and the malady drives her pen over her notebook.

"I've been thinking about you, Drew," the Pastor says. "I've been wondering how to help you – wondering just how I might support you and your mind. You've been a lost soul for so long, but now you've been found. And after some consideration, I know exactly what you require. Have I not always said 'love is a healing remedy'? You see, Drew, I believe it's time for you to form a meaningful romantic relationship here in Salvation. I believe love is what you're sorely missing. With that in mind, I think it's best that you take a partner – a wife."

Drew stutters.

The Pastor continues. "You'll be pleased to know that I have selected a partner for you. Someone who will bring out the best in you. Someone you can trust and grow with. Tonight, I will perform the ceremony. Your partner, ordained by me, is someone I like very much, and it's someone I believe you already know. She's proven herself to be capable. Congratulations, Drew, today, you and Megan are to be married."

Megan splutters, "But, Dad…"

"But nothing. Megan, I can see your relationship with Huxley isn't working. It's not healthy, it can never work. I have already given Huxley the news and partnered him with another. This is my will. You and Drew will be married right here, today. The ceremony will begin as soon as I've made the announcement. It will be done."

40

THE KITCHEN

The Common Room is quiet, lunch service has passed and only a few silver-haired men huddle around domino tiles. Hazel hurries passed them into the kitchen.

"Courtney!" she pleads in a whisper.

The room is empty.

Damnit! I need those keys!

She has no idea where else to look.

Maybe they keys are in here someplace.

She sets out on a hunt, looking over countertops, exploring closets and rummaging through drawers as quietly as she can. Her eyes drift over a sink filled with dishes, to where an apron is balled-up on a shelf. She unfurls it and finds the damp pockets are empty, but in the corner of her eye she sees a series of dark drops on the floor. They're small but numerous and they lead to the freezer. She can't resist following the trail.

A glance into the Common Room, the coast is clear. She walks to the freezer and lays her hands on its cold handle. The door opens with surprising ease, the freezing temperatures within chill her skin. Inside, a cold haze hangs in the air. She sees a faint outline form as the mist clears.

Oh my god!

She almost stumbles at the sight of Tom's naked torso, ice white and heavy, hanging in front of her. His face is tortured, begging and frozen. She backs away, trembling, unable to process it. She can't believe it's the same person she had breakfast with only yesterday. Courtney lies in a pool of blood below, clinging to the edge of the door frame with a blood red knife in her hand, her face decorated with iced tears.

Hazel's energy seeps from her chest and into her legs as full panic sets in. She means to run, but *something* is at her back.

It can't be.

A tattooed forearm wraps around her neck. It tenses and grips. She claws at it, swinging her elbows, but she can't breathe. Massive pressure in her head. Her feet lift off the floor.

Legs kicking the air.

A swirling in the ears.

Weakness in the arms.

Warm blood in the head.

Throbbing pulse, thick and short.

The taste of iron.

Tongue swollen in the mouth.

Can't breathe.

Darkness.

41

THE WEDDING

"Attention. Attention. Everyone
report to the Sermon Hall
immediately. It's with celebration
that I announce the marriage of Drew
Samuel and Megan Dwight. All must
join to witness the ceremony. Join
the happy couple in the Sermon Hall
immediately. That is all."

Jubilant people pour into the Sermon Hall. Megan blushes at
the sudden rush of attention as ladies flutter around her, smiling
and hugging. The dusty piano springs to life with a bright, off-
key melody, and Drew's surrounded by men offering
handshakes and congratulations.

"Boy, I knew you and her had a spark, I just knew it," Nick
says.

The hustle and bustle consume the betrothed. Megan
glances across the room towards Huxley, who's just walked to
the hall holding Judy's hand. Megan looks back at Drew. Her
expression is blank as she takes his hand and says, "We hardly
know each other, and we may not like each other very much,
but this is Father's will. So, it's our duty to embrace it, and I
will embrace it. We'll learn to love each other, and I will let
you be my husband."

Moments gather, accelerate, twist and turn. The discordant piano slows its dance to an inharmonious rendition of Ave Maria and before Drew can draw breath, the Pastor is at the lectern and the people have taken their seats.

"Dearly beloved," the Pastor begins, "we've already celebrated some very special occasions together here in Salvation. From arriving on our first night, to the birth of little Quincy, we now gather to witness a special union – the coming together of Drew and Megan."

The crowd cheers and the Pastor speaks warmly above the noise.

"While it is true that a man can be made strong with the support of love, it's equally true that a woman can find great power from the alliance of marriage. So it's my honor to wed these two today. I bless this union, so that it may be healthy and fruitful, so that it may serve Salvation greatly. There's nothing nobler or finer in the eyes of Father. While we all know what consequences can come from denying Father's will, we also all understand the beauty of his vision."

A woman in the front row wipe tears from her eyes.

"Let us begin. Do you, Megan Dwight, take this man, Drew Samuel, and pledge to be one half of a whole. To bear his children and serve Salvation together for the rest of your life and all eternity? Repeat after me. 'Father, I take this man, Drew Samuel'…"

"Father, I take this man, Drew Samuel."

"To be my partner in life forever."

"To be my partner in life forever."

Joyous celebration sweeps through the crowd, intensifying the fear flowing through Drew's veins.

"Drew Samuel, do you in turn accept the love of Megan in a union ordained by Father? Do you honor my will and accept her hand forever? And forsake all others besides her, Father and Salvation? Repeat after me. 'I, Drew Samuel, take this woman, Megan Dwight'…"

Drew can't think.

The crowd shuffle with disquiet.

"Drew, for all that is good, you *will* take this woman in life, so repeat after me… 'I, Drew Samuel, take this woman, Megan…'"

Drew looks over the crowd, the Pastor, to Megan.

"Say it." commands the Pastor.

"I, Drew Samuel…"

"Say it!"

"I Drew Samuel, take this woman, Hazel…"

Surprise lights the room. Drew's eyes grow wide with the shock of his own words and the crowd glares at him. Megan looks at the Pastor and they both swell with rage. She balls her fists.

Drews braces for impact.

"Father!" A yell comes from the doorway and all heads turn as Sid walks down the aisle, carrying Hazel on his shoulder.

"Oh my gosh!" says a voice in the crowd, triggering a ripple of excitement.

"Father, I'm sorry to interrupt – but I found this one snooping around where she don't belong." He lays Hazel on the floor and stands back.

Drew kneels at her side and checks for signs of life. "What did you do to her!"

The audience look to the Pastor and his eyes glow as he gathers his force and pounds on the lectern.

"How dare you motherfuckers deny my will! I have never in all my life seen such treachery! Well, I think we all know what needs to be done here! I think it's clear to all of us that these two motherfuckers need to pay a visit to the god-damn *Blue-eyed Monster*!"

Animated gasps and excited confusion stir the crowd, but Megan loses no time. She pounces on Drew, and the Planning Committee follow her lead. The blows fall at a wicked pace and Drew is unconscious before he hits the floor.

42

THE MONSTER

Hazel wakes up in complete darkness. It's cold. Her head throbs. Her hands are bound at her back and something's tied across her mouth. She can't see anything, but she can hear breathing on the other side of the abyss.

A ball of brilliant blue light sparks and vanishes. A cackle calls from the void.

"Mister Samuelssss…"

The blue flash reappears, ripping open the darkness, its flashing electric teeth illuminate Drew. He's bound and gagged, his eyes are bloody, and a bead of blood runs down his cheek.

The monster screams, "I take this man, Drew Samuel!" and bites down on Drew's chest. His body sizzles and tenses with unnatural power. The shock makes his body rigid and trembling. Hazel calls to him, but the fabric in her mouth reduces her voice to a strained muffle. More bites on Drew's chest, more convulsions, more calling his name, then the Blue-eyed Monster retreats into the gloom.

Drew's heavy, rapid breathing is the only sound in the dark.

With another fissure of light, the monster reappears at Drew's shoulder. It lunges and attacks again, and vicious sparks hiss and snap in contact with Drew's skin. He slumps forward and falls to the floor. Hazel shouts to him again, but she knows only the monster can hear her now. And she knows she's next.

"Hazel Cox," the beast whispers. The voice is low, crude, distorted. "Do you know just what you do to me?" The sizzling crack appears in front of her, flashing, chewing, and heating the air, moving closer in front her eyes. The monster's formless mouth spits branches of lightning, and it's razor heat is on her cheek.

"I see you around here. And all the time you do it to me."

She feels a cold hand touch her shoulder, as it slides down to her breasts. It lingers, squeezes and slithers lower, caressing her stomach and gliding down to her knees. She thrashes. The hand moves towards the edge of her gown and makes its way underneath.

She clamps her thighs and screams till her throat hurts, but the claw forces her legs open and begins to creep. Fingers stroke her inner thigh and crawl along her skin, moving higher, groping, pawing until it reaches the cotton of her underwear. A muffled protest is all she can do to resist as the beast pulls at her underwear.

"What is this?" the monster says.

Hazel's cell phone clatters to the floor. The monster reaches for it, and by a touch of its hand the screen comes to life, casting a white beam upwards and illuminating the Monster's face – the face of the Pastor.

Hazel lashes out a knee and strikes the Pastor in the head, toppling him to the ground. The phone falls out of his hand, its light is extinguished and once again she's plummeted into darkness.

"You're gonna be fucking sorry for that!" the Pastor says.

Her breathing is heavy and loud. She can't silence it. With her hands bound, she rises to her feet, sightless. With retreat impossible, she listens for the Pastor's breath and struggles against the ropes at her wrists. She takes a small step forward, then another, probing the area in front of her with her feet.

"O death, where is thy sting? O grave, where is thy victory?" the Pastor crawls on the floor, searching. "You're gonna dieeee…" he laughs.

She holds her breath to quell all noise. She can hear her heartbeat.

"I can hear it. I can hear your heart beating, Hazel, my sweet Hazel. Would you like to know what I'm going to do to you? Do you want to know what fun I'm going to have? Don't worry, when I'm done, Heaven's gate will be open, and I'll feed my church with your flesh."

The pulsing in Hazel's ears intensifies. She tries to block it out, tries to concentrate.

"Resist me and my angels will throw you into the fiery furnace, where there will be weeping and gnashing of teeth inside the doors of Hell. Come to me, Hazel!"

The scent of the Pastor's aftershave hits her on a rush of air as he swings a fist and misses. She kicks into the dark and makes partial contact.

"You bitch! So, you think you're a god?" He swings again, punching into the air.

She swings out a leg and makes direct contact. She kicks again and again, knocking the Pastor to the ground. The Pastor catches her foot and pulls her to the floor. She crashes down, landing on her tied hands. Pain shoots up her shoulders, and the Pastor is quick on her – beating her around the head. She throws a knee into his crotch, toppling him to the side. The struggle has loosened the bonds around her wrists, and she pulls against the ropes and fights her hands free.

Scrambling to her knees, she knocks an object across the floor. Reaching out, she grabs it. Deciphering it with her hands, she feels long metal pole with a plastic handle. She gets to her feet and swings it, beating the Pastor as he rises. She grips it tighter and beats him harder. Her finger stumbles on a button, and a blue bolt shoots from the tip of the pole.

Lit by its blue light, Hazel sees the Blue-eyed Monster is no more than a cattle prod. She pulls the trigger and zaps the Pastor in the chest with a long, unbroken shock. He cries a primal groan. She hits him with anther bolt, again and again and again – until no more sparks fly. The Pastor slumps to the floor. She drops the spent cattle prod, removes the gag from her mouth, and pulls up her underwear.

"What's the weather like in Hell, dickhead?"

The void is quiet again. The monster may have been vanquished, but she knows her escape from the darkness has not yet been won.

43

HAPPINESS IS A WARM GUN

"Drew!" she yells.

Sightless, Hazel feels her way across the floor, tracking the sound of Drew's faint, muzzled breathe. She finds his body, reaches for his face, and removes his muzzle. His breath is quick and short.

"I can't see anything!" he gasps.

"I know but try to hear me. It's Hazel. Are you OK?" She can feel the blood on his cheek.

"Hazel? Is that you, Hazel? It's no good, it's too dark for me to see, and I can't hear you.".

She pushes her lips against his.

"It's me," she says.

"Hazel." His forehead touches hers. "I just need a second, and I need light."

She fumbles at his back and unties his hands. He staggers to his feet.

"There has to be a light switch on one of these walls," he says, feeling his way across the room. "OK, wall, found. There has to be a switch around her somewhere."

With a click, the light come on, stinging her eyes. Drew's face is scuffed and bruised – blood has started to dry around his eye.

"This must be the Pastor's room," she says.

The room is similar to the other bedrooms, but unique in two ways: the door holds a key in its lock, and a desk sits at one side of the room.

The Pastor's body is doubled over on the floor in front of the desk. His gown is a mess of shiny black cloth.

"He dead?" asks Drew.

"Think so."

"Good."

The desk is neat and furnished with a writing mat, some letters, a notepad, and a plastic microphone.

"Drew," she says, "there's something you need to know. Courtney and Tom, I found them."

"Yeah?"

"I'm sorry... They're both dead. They were in the kitchen, in the freezer. Tom was... he was... His body has been cut up. And I think we've all been eating him. I think they served him for lunch! That's where the meat came from!"

Drew closes his eyes, lifts his hands to his face, and takes a long breath. "We need to tell everybody. We need to tell them what you saw."

"I know. And we'll show them what this place really is. Then everyone will want out of here. They'll have to open the door and let us go."

"I have a plan – bear with me." Drew moves towards the Pastor's desk and looks through the drawers.

"What are you looking for?"

"A weapon or anything we can use, just in case. The Pastor must have something around here, knowing what kind of man he was."

Hazel stares at the spent cattle prod on the floor. In the light, it's clearly a cheap farm tool. She picks it up to try its trigger again, no power. She scans the contents of the old notepad on the Pastor's desk and finds a handwritten series of notes. There's one from nurse Chamberlin, dated today.

"Father, I've wrestled with the views you have presented today. I keep coming back to the same view that revolutionary suicide is the only solution we have in the event of an invasion.

The United States government has unlimited supplies. We will not survive continuous skirmishes. I see bravado behind some of the comments in favor of fighting against an invasion. These voices assume that if we fight hard enough, we could protect you and the integrity of the group. I disagree – both the leader and the group would not survive – our enemy's power and resources are astronomical; our powers are limited.

The thing that disturbs me most about fighting is our lack of control over the consequences. After losing to an invading force, many of us would be taken and tortured – I worry that even I would break down. We are not familiar with the life of physical suffering like the brave peasants of China, Vietnam, and Russia are. Revolutionary suicide is our only option, especially in this regard.

Ultimately, I trust only you. The enemy is clever and that which would be fetched from our mouths would be calculated to harm the worldwide struggle of our movement. In a fight, we would not have control of which of us, and how many of us, would be taken in as captives. Though the strongest might kill themselves before being taken, the weakest – no matter what they might say in public meetings – would not kill themselves and they would be the first to talk. The problem of survivors after a conflict is not solved to my satisfaction. We don't have a solution; we cannot be sure that we won't leave half-alive children behind when the enemy is breathing down our back.

My proposal is the following; If at any point it appears that we will have to take the ultimate step, we prepare the people via the PA system by reading the words of strong assertive revolutionaries of the past. Our idea will face resistance due to its unfamiliarity. Awareness of this tactic should be taught in school classes, and it should be taught in sermons. When the time comes, and when all of our alternatives have been used up, we will meet as a group in the Sermon Hall, surrounded by highly trusted security members.

Names will be called off a list. People will be escorted to a place of dying (Common Room) by a strong personality who is loving, supportive but not sympathetic. They (victim/escort) are accompanied by two Blue Gowns. (I don't trust people to arrange their own death, but it can be arranged by outside pressure with no alternatives left.) At the place of dying, they are shot in the head, and if I do not believe they are definitely dead I will slit their throat with a scalpel. The bodies would be thrown outside. It might be advisable to blindfold the people before going to the death place, in that the blood and bodies remaining on the ground might increase agitation.

Any people who resist revolutionary suicide will do so because they want to save their own asses – they would make excellent captives for the enemy – saying anything they want under the illusion that they would be protected. These people must be the first to die.

The idea sickens me. At first, when we discussed fighting an invasion, I felt exhilarated by the idea of fighting. Though I'm nothing great with a gun, I knew I could do something to divert the enemy or give medical help to a fellow fighter – I can be active, hitting the enemy one way or another. There is nothing exhilarating about this new plan. It's horrible, but it's safe and I know you will see its virtue.

-Nurse Chamberlin"

"Drew!" shouts Hazel, pulling at his shoulder. "They're planning to kill everyone! Something about an invasion. They're going to tell everyone to commit revolutionary suicide, and they're going to shoot them in the Common Room."

"It's a good thing we're getting out of here, then." Drew tosses a few books out of the desk's draws, "What is this?" He holds up a sleek black handgun. "This might come in useful as insurance against the Blue Gowns. I've never used a gun before, but I'm glad we have it."

"What's your plan?"

"Hurricane, or no hurricane, we're leaving. You're right. I have to take responsibility for my life. The lying to myself, the hiding every day – it stops now. I have hopes and dreams and that counts for something. It's time to get back to reality, if it still exists out there. I want another shot at life, so we're going to get everyone in the Sermon Hall, then we hit them with the truth about Tom and Courtney."

"But what about the Planning Committee?"

"I have an idea, and it starts with that microphone on the desk, it must broadcast to the loudspeaker system." He nods at the plastic announcer mic on the desk. "Here we go." He leans over the mic, swallows hard and pushes the button on its base:

```
"Sid  and  all  Blue  Gowns  report  to
Father's room. Everyone else report to
the  Sermon  Hall  immediately.  Repeat,
everyone  else  report  to  the  Sermon
Hall."
```

Drew puts the plastic body of the microphone against the edge of the desk and pushes against it, snapping it in two.

"Come on." He grabs Hazel by the hand, and they run to the corridor. As he passes the door, he removes the key from the lock and they hide around the corner, just out of view. Footsteps come close, then disappear into the Pastor's room. The door slams and there's a cry of "Oh my God!". Drew races to the door, slips the key in the lock and turns it, trapping the Planning Committee inside.

"OK. That'll buy us some time. We have one shot at this."

They rush to the Sermon Hall.

44

THE MASTER KEY

A chattering crowd chokes the Sermon Hall corridor and pours inside. Hazel and Drew push their way through the crush and race to the lectern. The congregation watch with surprise as the couple approach the microphone, but Hazel and Drew leave no time for questions. While many are still searching for seats, Drew starts his address.

"I've gathered you for an emergency meeting. Please listen carefully to what I am about to say, as we don't have much time." He takes a breath, and without apology, hits them with the news.

"Your Pastor is dead."

The crowd startles. Some recoil and cry with the instant sting of grief, some stand and yell "No!". Others look about with full faced astonishment.

"Your Pastor was lying to you all," Hazel adds. "Don't you see what this place is? It's a prison. You were his captives, but now you're free!"

Charlie limps into the room, the last to enter.

Drew adds his voice to Hazel's petition. "Not only did he manipulate you and beat you, but people went missing – Tom and Courtney. I know you remember them. Hazel found them both dead in the kitchen freezer! Go and see for yourselves. And all that meat you ate? Guess what, it was human, it was Tom. You all ate Tom's body, and your Pastor killed him because he stood up for himself. Then he fed him to you. Do you understand what I'm saying? We all need to get out of here. We all need to leave now!"

The people look stunned, each holding their own expression of horror. Some shake their heads, some cry into their hands.

Barbara lifts a hand above the sea of three hundred red gowns.

"May I say something?" she says.

"Yes, please," Hazel says.

Barbara rises to her feet and speaks with slow, difficult comprehension.

"So, what you are saying is that Father killed Tom? And your friend Courtney too? And what we have all been eating was meat from Tom's body?"

"Yes! That's exactly what we're saying," Drew says.

"Well, um, it seems to me that, if Father killed Tom and your friend, all I can figure is that they must have been bad people. They must've been trying to hurt us. I don't agree with the bad things you said about Father. Father would only kill if it was right to do it. And I didn't know that what I ate was a human, but I tell you all what, it sure was good eatin'..."

A laugh breaks the silence and one by one, the crowd chuckle.

"Oh, *yeah*, sister!" encourages an older man.

"Tell them, honey! Say it," shouts another.

A second woman rises to her feet. "You know, if Father wanted us to eat people, and now he's dead, I think he would want us to do the only fair and right thing and follow his example. With that said, I think the only thing to do is to eat Father's sacred body. I think that's what he would have wanted."

An applause is triggered by a cry of "Truth!".

Drew recoils. Hazel is pale and speechless.

Another voice yells, "I bet he would taste so damn good. Imagine, y'all."

"Wait, wait!" comes another shout. "How did Father die?"

Hazel shakes her head. "You don't need to know that."

"You!" cries a voice. "You did this, didn't you? You killed Father!"

Chaos breaks out as the idea spreads. People stand, shout, stomp, and point with angry animation. The air thick with noise.

Charlie, sitting alone at the back, stands. With his mouth and eyes still swollen blue and puffy red, he waves his hands in the air.

"Look, everybody! Shut up! Shut up, for the love of Father, shut up."

The rabble stops and turns to Charlie with a collective disaffection.

"Since day one," he says, wincing and touching his swollen lip, "I felt like my place was here with you and Father, but for some reason, Father never accepted me. I never knew why that was. I tried and tried, but now I understand. He was just testing me to get me ready for *this* moment. And now I know what I gotta do. I know that I need to prove myself, and right now I'm going to do just that. I don't need no blue gown to take care o' this shit. I'm gonna take control right here, right now and avenge our father."

He emerges from the back, first limping, then striding. He grows taller and stronger with every step. The crowd break into their war call. The noise is a piercing unmelodious roar. The discordant throng gathers behind Charlie and marches on towards Hazel and Drew, trapping them at the lectern. Five men join Charlie at the head of the crowd, moving in for the kill, encouraged by high-pitched noise and screeching laughter and yells of "Avenge our father!" and "Kill those motherfuckers!" and "I bet that bitch Hazel tastes real nice!"

"Look!" implores Hazel, "He's not what he says he is! He's no God! He claimed to see all and know all. He claims to see pain and cure it – but he never realized that Drew is almost deaf! How can you explain that?"

Charlie spits blood. "Fuck you, bitch."

The crowd marches on.

Drew pulls out the Pastor's gun. He holds it high into the air, but the threat does nothing to halt the advance or to diminish their appetite for vengeance. He fires a warning shot into the ceiling. Concrete dust scatters over the crowd. They stop.

Hazel pounces on the microphone.

"Your Pastor was going to kill you all! I have proof. Tom and Courtney are dead because of him. And I have this letter right here, explaining how he was going to murder all of you."

The crowd press closer in a tide of red.

Hazel and Drew back away, step after step.

Their backs press against the cold concrete wall.

They steal a last glance at each other.

"Stay back!" Drew shouts, with his last pluck of courage. "I have enough bullets to take down at least a dozen of you fuckers!"

"More bodies, more meat! You can't take us all down, bitch!" Charlie shouts.

Drew shields Hazel and aims his gun at kill height. With the mob close, he can't miss. "Once the crowd tastes lead, they'll change their mind," he shouts. His finger settles on the trigger. He has never shot a man before. He squeezes the cold metal.

Empty chambers click.

The gun's only bullet, one the Pastor must have reserved for himself for when the need became dire, is lodged harmlessly in the ceiling of his Sermon Hall.

Drew prepares to fight. He can't save Hazel, he can't save himself, but he can die trying. The first punch thrown his way is easily dodged.

"Look at the corridor!" Hazel shouts.

Drew counters a second blow and glances at the doorway. In the corridor he sees a thin column of light on the wall. The vertical slither of gold grows and stretches across the walkway and fills Salvation's entrance with brilliant light. A loud metallic boom ripples through the Sermon Hall, distracting the battalion of red.

Drew and Hazel push through the mob. Through the punches, kick and scratches, they push with speed and violence towards the light in the corridor. The door, the blessed exit, is open, and yellow sunshine streams over a small, silhouetted figure at the threshold. They sprint towards the exit and the mysterious figure moves aside.

Outside, cars zoom along a far, unseen highway, and birds sing in blossoming trees under a pastel sky. The ground is damp and green underfoot. The sun is warm on their faces.

They stop and look back to the door. There stands Mother, solemn and still, almost floating in the sunlight. She faces the horizon with her eyes closed and her head high, her yellow dress moving gently in the breeze. Her presence holds back the crowd.

"Am I not your mother?"

The crowd behind her nod and murmur, moving restlessly, ready to pounce.

"For too long we have tried. And we have tried so very hard. For too long we have listened without action. For too long we have made easy choices." She lifts her sorrowful expression to the sky, as if the universe and all its stars had called her name.

Hazel backs away.

Drew yells, "You had the key to the door this whole time, didn't you! You could have stopped all of this."

"No, dear, no," mother says, "You see, the only lock on this door was Father's words. And what were Father's words to you last night?" She pauses. "Ah, yes, he said, 'This is the last time I'm going to save your ass.' Well, I'm not Father, and since he's gone and since I'm woman of kindness, it's only fair that I give you and Hazel... a head start."

The crowd resume their awful ululation. Hazel and Drew look at each other.

Mother counts down.

"Ten... nine... eight... seven..."

Drew releases a long-held breath and whispers, "Time to run".

They turn and dash and rush and fall and panic and sprint with primal focus. They speed past Drew's old Buick, ruing the knowledge that without keys the faithful car would be a coffin for them both. They race through the daylight and into the woods with the dreadful melody of Salvation's war call at their backs.

45

THE END

Shades of memories. Snapshots of sound. The blurry corridor between sleeping and waking. Mary is here, smiling after an argument. "If we cannot live in peace then let us die in peace..." The smell of gunpowder. Shouting, yelling. A voice. "Oh, how very much I have loved you..." Crying in anguish. The ecstasy of a crowd. "How very much I have tried to give you the good life..." Fighting. Confusion. Reverberation in the corridor. "But in spite of all that I have tried, two people, with their lives, have made our lives impossible." Then peace.

In the early hours of Tuesday morning on the 23rd of March 2021, Stephen wakes up blinking at a concrete ceiling. There's a red gown on his body, and his feet are bare. In a strange dark room, he finds his boots, two other beds, a few medical devices, and a space heater. He gets to his feet. His legs are bruised and sore, but he has enough mobility to wander out of his room into the narrow, gloomy space outside: a corridor. The silence here is profound. According to a fragment of memory, this environment would usually be rich with noise and activity, but nothing stirs now.

Confused and afraid, he experiences what it feels like to be the last man on earth. The smell hit him first. Like old meat left out during a hot summer. The stench hangs in the air, and he can't turn his nose from it. Even when breathing through the fabric of his gown, the odor makes him heave. He walks into an open hall to where bodies line the floor, lying on their chests and clad in red robes. Some are locked in an embrace, as if in sleep, others are contorted with struggle.

Corpses pack the area outside the kitchen. A few appeared to have been trying to escape but had been killed in the process. There were many, many bodies, too many to count. Stephen finds a letter perched on a table:

Momma,

We came to Salvation for shelter, not just from the hurricane, but from the turbulence of life itself. Some may not understand that, but many will. For those who come after us and want an explanation, I hope they look to their own lives and to society for answers. I hope they ask themselves, is this really good enough? Is this the life they wanted?

Salvation lived and died for our ideals of brotherhood, co-operation, justice and equality, ideals that society outside these walls would not let live and be real.

I hope they look at Salvation and see what we tried to do – This was a monument to life, [cross-out] to the renewal of the human spirit that had been broken by a system of exploitation & injustice. Look at all that was built by a beleaguered people. I know we didn't want this kind of ending – we wanted to live, to shine, to bring light to a world that is dying for a little love. Many will leave behind loved ones. I am grateful for this opportunity to bear a bitter witness with you.

Ours are a beautiful people, a brave people. I am not afraid. I am calm in this hour of our collective leave-taking. As I write these words, people are silently amassed and ready for relief. We are a long-suffering people. [cross-out] Many of us are weary of the long search and the long struggle.

It's sad that we could not let our light shine in truth, unclouded by the demons of circumstances. People are hugging each other now, embracing, we are hurrying – [cross-out] we do not want to be captured. We want to bear witness at once. I see hugging and kissing and tears and silence and joy in a long line.

Momma, you, like many of us, are now dead. With each moment, another passes over to peace. We are begging only for understanding. It will take more than small minds, reporters' minds, to fathom these events. Something must come of this. Beyond all the circumstances surrounding the immediate event, someone can perhaps find the symbolic, the eternal [cross-out] in this moment – the meaning of a people and their struggle – I wish I had time to write it all down. Someone else will have to write this story.

We did not want it this way. No matter what view anyone takes of us, perhaps the most relevant truth is that our movement was filled with outcasts and the poor *who were looking for something they couldn't find in society.*

If nobody understands, it matters not. People may think that we are brainwashed, but they are the robots. I am ready to die, and to join you. Darkness settles over Salvation on its last day on earth. No more pain, no more pain for us, but I hope people will ask themselves – Will the world ever be ready for peace and solidarity?

I love you Momma. Dad, I'm coming home,
– Oscar Hinchcliffe

It is said that he who goes to salvation and leaves, comes back mad. Stephen knows if this is true. He read the letter and saw all there was to see, and he limped away.

He found the spare key for his pickup in the car's sun visor and turned the engine over. It started first time.

"Trusty ol' Red…"

He reached for his phone, put it on charge and charted a course back through the woodland trail. As soon as a slither of signal hit his cell, he dialed 999.

'How long have we been out here? I'm too hungry to go on, tell me we're close." Drew falters to his knees. His gown is torn, dirty and irritating to the skin in the daylight heat.

"Get up," Hazel says, wearily, "We can't be far now, I swear we've been going in circles for about two days, but I can hear the sound of cars is getting louder. I think there's a road this way."

Through a fence of trees, Drew spies blue, red and white cars zooming along.

"Over there!" he yells, throwing himself through the overgrowth onto the tarmac.

"Look out!' screams Hazel.

A speeding car swerves around him and screeches to a halt. The driver jumps out.

"You maniac! I almost killed you! What the hell do you think you're doing!"

Hazel comes running, "Sir! Sir! You have to help us."

Despite their protests, authorities sent Drew and Hazel back to Salvation to help identify bodies. The media were quick on the scene and a frenzy of worldwide attention was waiting for them. The body count was 298. Nurse Chamberlin, Pastor Quincy Gordon and baby Quincy could not be found. Drew and Hazel were suspected, they were accused, they had no alibi, and before they could move on, they had to prove their innocence. Look out for The Shelter: Redemption coming 2023.

* * *

Thank you for reading The Shelter. I hope you enjoyed Drew and Hazel's journey towards doom as much as I did. If you enjoyed this, I think you'll like **Mika Ito**, it's an exciting new action thriller. **Turn the page to find more...**

Don't miss this up-and-coming action thriller!

MIKA ITO

British investigative journalist Dylan Solly is in Japan to cover the trial of three infamous Yakuza kingpins, but he has a nagging feeling that something's wrong. This will not be a normal assignment, and today will not be a normal day. He visits the park, hoping a stroll will calm his nerves, but collapses on the grass.

That's just the start of his trouble.

Mika Ito, a local schoolteacher, comes to his aid. Minutes later, an earthquake hits, followed by a monstrous tsunami. The impact is devastating, and a major nuclear emergency is declared.

Now, they have no choice but to lean on each other and flee. As they head north, they fall in love. But this relationship is so dangerous it might just destroy them both.

Turn the page to read the first chapter...

MIKA ITO

CHAPTER ONE

It was 11 a.m. when Dylan Solly collapsed in Yonomori Park, and no matter what, he'd unlikely ever forget the rhythm of that cold March Friday morning. The day had started easy, but a call from his editor picked up the beat.

'Not again, Sam.'

'I know it's a lot earlier than we discussed, but I've got nothing for the next issue so I need your report ASAP.'

Dylan fumbled with the ring hanging from his necklace. 'The Notorious Three trial hasn't even started yet, and these guys are way above the usual Yakuza criminal enterprise. This thing goes deep and international, so it's worth taking our time. If we do this right, it'll be another award winner.'

'I'm sorry, no. Look, you'll get the story – I know you will. You always find a way. And, yes, there's a lot of ground to cover on this one but I can get Kasper on the next plane to Japan to help you with the research. Let me send you an assistant—'

'No. You'll get your story.'

Dylan hung up, reached for his cigarettes and slipped a notebook into his pocket. Then he grabbed his wallet and his old Nikon and headed out into the cool air of the park, where the melody of his late-morning anxiety climaxed.

A jagged scar appeared across his vision, narrowing the view of the bright blossoms. The pressure in his skull built. He pitched forward and the camera slipped from his hands. Newly cut grass squashed under his palms as he met the ground.

He rolled onto his back.

The sun transformed into a halo of scattered phosphorus pink, violet and gold. That's when he saw her, looming over on him, blocking the harsh light. While rings of purple orbited her, Dylan passed out.

MIKA ITO – COMING AUGUST 2022

Sign up to my newsletter at https://peterfoley.co.uk to find out more about my upcoming books and follow me on social media @thepeterfoley.

See you there

A NOTE FROM THE PUBLISHER

Thank you for reading this book. If you enjoyed it please do consider leaving a review on Amazon to help others find it too.

I hate typos. This book has been rigorously edited and proofread, but sometimes mistakes do slip through. If you have spotted a typo, please do let me know and I'll get it amended.

peter@peterfoley.co.uk

www.peterfoley.co.uk

@thepeterfoley

Printed in Great Britain
by Amazon

17089866R00135